As he came closer, the realization struck her like lightning.

She hadn't seen Mason Harrington in almost fifteen years. Oh, she'd wondered about him almost every day. But she'd refused to let her curiosity turn into anything more. After all, she imagined she was the last person Mason ever wanted to contact him.

It looked like the years had been good to him. Even at this distance, she could spot the telltale features she'd found so attractive: the dark blond hair cropped close at the sides but leaving just enough length on the top to showcase its inherent wave; large hands rough from working but with long fingers that could play her like the most delicate of strings; the square shape of his jaw that belied the soft curve of his full bottom lip.

He was even taller now, filled out and muscular in a way that made her uncomfortably aware of him. As did the piercing blue gaze that found her with unerring accuracy. But it was the signature black cowboy hat that he swung up onto his head that was the nail in her coffin, confirming that she faced the boy she had wronged.

And now he was every inch a man.

Dear Reader,

I grew up on a farm and had a horse as a teenager (along with goats, cows, chickens and various house pets). Nothing on the scale of my Desire characters, but there was a certain peacefulness in being out in nature that much, a certain connection that can only be felt when caring for an animal's very existence. The circle of life as you attend births, nurse them through illnesses, watch out the window as they play and bury them with lots of tears. It's a very different life from my current suburban one.

That's why I'm excited to visit horse-racing country with the Harrington brothers! These men know the land, the animals, and the women who can give them exactly what they (think!) they want. Too bad for them love doesn't always play fair...

I love to hear from my readers! You can email me at readdaniwade@gmail.com or follow me on Facebook. As always, news about my releases is easiest to find through my author newsletter, which you can sign up for through my website at www.daniwade.com.

Enjoy!

Dani

DANI WADE

REINING IN THE BILLIONAIRE

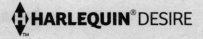
HARLEQUIN® DESIRE

Recycling programs
for this product may
not exist in your area.

ISBN-13: 978-0-373-83829-5

Reining in the Billionaire

Copyright © 2017 by Katherine Worsham

Printed in U.S.A.

Dani Wade astonished her local librarians as a teenager when she carried home ten books every week—and actually read them all. Now she writes her own characters, who clamor for attention in the midst of the chaos that is her life. Residing in the southern United States with a husband, two kids, two dogs and one grumpy cat, she stays busy until she can closet herself away with her characters once more.

Books by Dani Wade

Harlequin Desire

His by Design
Reining in the Billionaire

Mill Town Millionaires

A Bride's Tangled Vows
The Blackstone Heir
The Renegade Returns
Expecting His Secret Heir

Visit her Author Profile page at Harlequin.com, or daniwade.com, for more titles.

I'm very blessed in this life to have a wonderful mother-in-law, who I watch give herself tirelessly to those around her every day. Kay, thank you for all you do for us. These books would not happen without the love, encouragement and sheer physical support you gift to me and our family day after day. I love you.

One

Finding out that the old Hyatt estate was available for purchase immediately—cash buyers only—had to be the biggest triumph Mason Harrington had ever experienced. After all, how many people got to fulfill their life's goal of owning a horse farm and get the revenge they'd ached for—all in one unexpectedly easy move?

"The foreclosure was just approved and finalized through our corporate offices," the bank manager was saying from across the polished expanse of his desk. His worried expression made him look more like a concerned grandfather than a businessman. "The family hasn't even been notified yet. There simply hasn't been time—"

"I'll be happy to handle that part for you," Mason

heard himself say. *Oops! Was that too much?* From the look on the manager's face, probably. The nudge from his brother confirmed it.

Mason subtly leaned out of reach from his brother's sharp elbow, ignoring the creak of his leather chair. Kane might resent Daulton Hyatt for his role in ruining their father's reputation in this town, but Mason had been at ground zero for the man's nuclear meltdown.

He'd never forget the humiliation Daulton had dished out with satisfaction…or the pain of having EvaMarie watch without defending him.

If the memories made him a little mouthy…

"I have to say that the foreclosure went through against my wishes. I'd hoped to help EvaMarie turn things around," the manager said with a frown that deepened the lines on his aged face.

"Why EvaMarie?" Kane asked. "Wouldn't it be Daulton Hyatt who needed the help?"

The man's eyes widened a little as he watched them from across the desk. After a moment, he said, "I'm sorry. I spoke out of turn. I didn't mean to discuss personal details about my customers." He lowered his gaze to the printed paper before him. Mason had found the foreclosure notice on a local website. The bank hadn't wasted any time trying to recoup its loss. "But I just don't feel comfortable—"

"That doesn't matter now. The bank has already listed the property," Mason cut in. "Look, we are offering more than the asking price, cash in hand. Do we need to contact someone at the corporate offices ourselves?" Surely they'd be happy to take the Harrington money.

Mason could tell by the look on the manager's face that he most certainly did not want that to happen. But Mason would if he had to…

"We can have the money transferred here by this afternoon," Kane added. "Our offer is good for only an hour at that price. Do we have a deal?"

Mason's body tightened, silently protesting the idea of walking away, but his brother knew exactly what he was doing. Still, the thought of losing this opportunity chafed. The waffling manager was obviously trying to look out for the family, as opposed to the strangers before him, but right now Mason didn't give a damn about the Hyatts.

He cared only about making them pay for striking out at Mason and his family all those years ago.

He couldn't help but wonder how EvaMarie would look when he told her to get out of her family home…

Slowly, reluctantly, the older man nodded. "Yes. I guess this really is out of my hands now." He stood, straightening his suit jacket and tie as if steadying himself for a particularly unpleasant task. "If you'll excuse me a moment, I'll get my secretary started on the paperwork."

And he would no doubt call corporate while he went outside the office, Mason suspected, but it wasn't going to do him any good. What the Harrington brothers wanted, they often got. Usually it was from sheer bullheadedness. This time, though, they had their inheritance to back them up.

Money did open doors, indeed.

Mason still missed his dad, who had passed away about six months ago. It had been just the three of them for most of Mason's life, and they'd all been really tight. Learning of their father's cancer had been hard.

But it had only been the first surprise.

The fact that their mother had been the debutante daughter in a very wealthy family in a neighboring state had never been a secret to the boys. She'd died of brain cancer when Mason was around seven. He remembered so little about her, except how good she'd smelled as she cuddled with him and the silky softness of her hair. He would brush it for her sometimes, after she got sick, because it soothed her and often got rid of the headaches she frequently had.

Still, she'd been gone a long time. It had never occurred to either of the boys that she had left something behind for them. Hell—something? This wasn't just *something*, it was a fortune. Their father's careful money management had paid off in big ways, and he'd grown their already substantial inheritance into a monumental sum. Mason couldn't even think of the money in real dollar amounts, it was so excessive.

After all, sometimes they'd had to scrape the bottom of the barrel growing up. Like when Mason had lost his job at the Hyatt estate. They'd had to move back to his mother's hometown. Times had already been tough. Little had he and Kane known, their dad had been going without while planning for their future.

And their future was now.

After the secret came out, Mason had asked his father why he hadn't used some of the money to make life easier for him, for them. He'd said he never wanted to prove their mother's parents right—they'd always said he'd married her for money.

The brothers had been around horses all their lives. Their father had been a horse trainer with an excellent reputation for creating winners. He'd taught them everything he knew. They'd also both learned a lot from working in some of the best stables in the area, along with raising their own horses and cattle. Now, finally, they had the capital to purchase and establish their very own racing stables.

Oh, and get back at EvaMarie Hyatt for almost ruining his family at the same time.

"That look on your face has me damn worried," Kane said, studying him hard.

Mason stood, pacing the space that was relatively generous for a bank office but still left Mason feeling cramped. "I can't believe this is finally happening."

"You know Dad wouldn't want us to get back at the Hyatts for what happened almost fifteen years ago, right?"

It may have been close to fifteen years ago, but to Mason, the wounds and anger were as fresh as yesterday. Kane thought of it as a teenage crush, but Mason knew he had loved EvaMarie with everything he had at the time. Otherwise, it wouldn't still hurt so damn much.

"Yep, I know." But he could live with that. Simply

seeing the shock on EvaMarie's face—and that dictator daddy of hers—would be worth a little blackening on his soul.

Right?

"Are you saying you've changed your mind?" he asked Kane.

His brother was silent, thinking before he answered. Mason admired that about Kane—it was a trait he lacked. Mason jumped first and worried about the consequences later. But as a team, their differences worked in their favor...mostly.

Kane turned to meet his gaze, his expression harder than before. "Nah. I say, go for it. But just a little warning, Mason—"

Mason groaned. "Aren't we a little old for you to jump into big brother mode again?"

"I am your big brother, but that's not it." He gave Mason a level look. "You need to keep in mind that there might be a good reason that they've lost the estate. They may not care what happens to it or who has it. I haven't heard any rumors about them financially except that they were downsizing a while back."

He shrugged at Mason's raised brows. "So I kept tabs. But we're out of the loop, except for a few old friends." He shrugged, his suit still looking out of place to Mason. They were used to flannel shirts and sturdy jeans. Dressing up wasn't the norm...but considering where this inheritance was taking them, they'd better get used to it.

Kane shook his head. "I don't know. I just have a feeling this isn't going to play out like you want it to."

Mason thought back to his awed impression of the Hyatt estate when he was a know-it-all eighteen-year-old. The opulence, the care EvaMarie's mother had put into every little touch. That house had been her life. Not that Mason had been allowed to see it. Officially, he'd seen it only once. He'd been told to take some papers to Daulton Hyatt at the big house. EvaMarie's mother had trailed after him, anxious in case he tracked manure on her antique rugs.

As though he was too much of a heathen to know how to wipe his feet. The only other time he'd been inside, there hadn't been a parent in sight.

"You may be right," Mason conceded, trying to shake the memories away. "But trust me, they care. I remember that much all too well." And he was gonna use what he knew about them to his every advantage.

It paid to know thine enemy.

EvaMarie Hyatt didn't have a clue who was driving up to the house in a luxury sedan followed by a shiny new pickup truck. But as she spied out her bedroom window on the second floor, she fervently wished that whoever it was would go back from whence they came.

After all, she was sweaty and gross after hanging insulation inside the old dressing room between her suite and the next. Plus, she had a headache pounding hard enough between her temples to rival a jackhammer. And she was the only one here willing to answer the door.

Still, she smiled with the satisfaction of knowing

all of her hard work would be perfect for what she had in mind.

But this wasn't the time for lingering admiration of her handiwork. She had to get herself in gear and head their visitors off at the pass. She scurried down the back stairs, hyperaware of her parents' location. They'd be interested too, but she knew good and well they wouldn't come outside.

It was so sad to see her once social butterfly parents now housebound. Their secrecy and embarrassment made EvaMarie's responsibilities that much harder…and much more painful.

She made it to the side entrance just as the vehicles parked. Unexpected nerves tingled through her as she attempted to smooth her hair into some semblance of order. Maybe her parents were rubbing off on her…or the isolation of taking care of every last detail of their lives was turning her into a hermit.

To her surprise, the bank manager stepped out of the first vehicle, his pristine suit making her all too aware of her dust-covered T-shirt and sweatpants. But it was the driver of the truck who confounded her.

She studied him as the two men approached across the now cracking driveway. He was a stranger, yet familiar for some reason. There was something about the cocky set of his shoulders, the confidence of his stride. As he came closer, the realization struck her like lightning.

She hadn't seen Mason Harrington in nearly fifteen years. Oh, she'd wondered about him almost every day since then. But she'd refused to let her curiosity turn into anything more. After all, she imagined she was the last person Mason ever wanted to contact him.

It looked like the years had been good to him. Even at this distance, she could spot the telltale features she'd found so attractive: the dark blond hair cropped close at the sides, but leaving just enough length on the top to showcase its inherent wave; large hands rough from working but with long fingers that could play her like the most delicate of instruments; the square shape of his jaw that belied the soft curve of his full bottom lip.

He was even taller now, filled out and muscular in a way that made her uncomfortably aware of him. As did the piercing blue gaze that found her with unerring accuracy. But it was the signature black cowboy hat that he swung up onto his head that was the nail in her coffin, confirming that she faced the boy she had wronged.

And now he was every inch a man.

Mason Harrington was someone she certainly didn't want near the house…or within miles of her father. Rushing forward despite her nerves clenching her stomach, she ignored the bombshell and focused on the manager. "Clive," she said, "what can I do for you?"

"EvaMarie, I'm afraid I have some bad news."

She wanted to look at Mason, see if he knew what was going on. Which was silly. Of course he did or he wouldn't be here. "I thought we had everything straightened out last month?" Oh, goodness. Please let this not be what she feared most.

"Well, I'm afraid corporate overruled us. As I mentioned then, everything has to be approved through them."

Her breath caught for a moment, then she forced herself to speak. "But I thought you said you knew enough people up there to get them to listen."

"I know, honey. Apparently I wasn't quite persuasive enough. I was going to call today, but got—" he glanced at the silent man next to him "—sidetracked."

EvaMarie hugged herself as her heart pounded in her chest. Nausea washed through her. She'd been alone through a lot of hard times over the past five years, but right now she wondered if there was a person alive who wouldn't let her down. "What does that mean?"

Mason stepped forward, his boots scraping across the driveway. "It means I'm the new owner of the Hyatt estate."

His voice had deepened. This was a man speaking. A man taking away what he had to know meant the world to her. She couldn't even look him in the eye. Turning back to Clive, she struggled not to beg. "I just need a little more time—"

"Too late."

Mason's harsh words made her cringe, but she tried to focus only on Clive. Breathlessly she pushed the words out. "But the mares will foal—"

Clive stepped forward, cutting off her view of

Mason with a hand on her shoulder. "You know it won't cover more than a few payments," he said, his voice low and firm, even though his touch was gentle. "Then you'll be behind again. You've done the best you could, EvaMarie, but we both know you're only delaying the inevitable. It's time. Time to let go."

She shook her head, the words ringing in her ears. Time to admit defeat—to Mason Harrington. Her father would rather die.

For a moment, she almost gave in to the tears that had plagued her for the last six months. She glanced over at the quiet, still barn in the distance. The surrounding lush trees had sheltered her since she'd first walked. The lake in the distance had seen her learn to swim and fish. The rolling hills had been her playground in her youth, her solace as she'd gotten older. Her mind conjured up memories of a time long ago when the picture before her had been bustling with employees, and horses, and visitors.

Not anymore. *No matter how hard she tried.*

Every time she'd thought she was making progress, yet another setback would stomp on her efforts. But this one was the crowning glory.

Now she zeroed in on Mason, surprised by his smug *I won* look. Obviously, he could remember a lot about this place, too. Part of her ached that he still hated her enough to find taking her home from her a worthy challenge. But a part that she didn't want to acknowledge found a tiny bit of solace in the fact that she could still touch him in some way.

She'd never be able to admit all the ways he'd

changed her, even after he'd been gone. The thought was enough to have her dragging her stoic expression back into place, covering her true emotions, all of the frustration and pain she'd dealt with since he'd left, since her father became ill.

She felt so alone.

"So when do we have to be out?" she murmured, struggling to be practical. She wouldn't think right now about how it would feel, leaving the only home she'd ever known. That would lead to the breakdown she wanted to avoid.

Mason stepped fully into view, muscling his way around the bank manager. How he'd heard her, she wasn't sure. "As soon as possible would be great. You can work that out with Clive here, but first, I'd like to look over my purchase, please."

If she hadn't been struggling already, his complete lack of compassion would have taken her breath away. EvaMarie looked at the smug man, seeing again the few traces of the boy she'd loved with all her heart, the boy she'd given her body to, even though she'd known she couldn't keep him—and wished she had the courage to punch him in the face.

Two

Mason's crude satisfaction at besting EvaMarie and her family quickly transformed to dismay as he followed her into the house.

Bare. That's the word that came to mind as he looked around the entryway and beyond. It was like a gorgeous painting stripped of all its details, all the way down to the first broad brushstrokes covering the canvas. The basic structure was still there. The silver-leafed cabinetry, the crystal doorknobs, the delicate ironwork. But a lot of the decorative china and porcelain figures and landscape paintings he remembered from that long ago day had disappeared, leaving behind bare shelves and walls that projected an air of sadness.

They had entered the house through a side door,

the same one Mason had been let into fifteen years ago. The long hallway took them past the formal dining room and a parlor, then a couple of now empty rooms until they came to a sunken area facing the back of the house. Apparently the family used this as a cozier living room, if one could call the massive, hand-carved limestone fireplace and equally impressive Oriental carpeting "cozy."

Upon closer inspection, the once pristine furniture had a few worn corners. But weirdly enough, what impacted Mason the most was the flowers. Not the ones in the overrun garden outside the wall of windows, but the ones in the vase on the table behind the sofa as they entered the room.

He vividly remembered the large sprays of flowers in intricate vases from his first visit, impressed as he had been with their color and beauty. They'd been placed every few feet in the hall and several in each of the rooms he'd glanced into and entered. But this was the first flower vase he'd seen today: a simple cut-glass one. Inside was an arrangement of flowers that looked like they'd been cut from the wild gardens. Pretty, but they were obviously not the designer arrangements of hothouse blooms he remembered.

Boy, the privileged had truly come down in the world.

Glancing over to the couple seated near the fireplace, he recognized EvaMarie's parents, even though they'd aged. Mrs. Hyatt was dressed for visitors. Mason would expect nothing less, though her silk shirt and carefully quaffed hair denoted a woman who hadn't faced the reality of her situation.

The pearls were a nice touch though.

"What's going on?" Daulton asked, his booming voice still carrying enough to echo slightly on the eardrums. "Clive, why are you here?"

The bank manager shook hands with the couple, then stepped back a bit to allow EvaMarie closer. Mason had thought he'd want to see this part, to witness the lowering of the high-and-mighty Hyatts. After all, they'd orchestrated the moment that had brought his own family's downfall.

Yet somehow, he couldn't bring himself to close in, to gain an angle that allowed him to see EvaMarie's face as she gave her family the news that their lives were about to change. Afraid he was softening, he forced himself to stand tall, knees braced for the coming confrontation. He forced himself to remember how his father must have felt that day when he'd had to tell Mason and his brother that he was fired from the position he'd held for ten years at the insistence of Daulton Hyatt.

That hadn't been pretty either.

"Mom, Dad, um." EvaMarie's voice was so soft Mason almost couldn't hear it. Yet he could feel the vibration in his body. EvaMarie's voice was unique—even huskier than it had been when she was young. She'd grown into a classic Kathleen Turner voice that Mason was going to completely and totally ignore. "The bank has sold the estate."

Mrs. Hyatt's gasp was quickly drowned beneath

Daulton's curse. "How is that possible?" he demanded. "Clive, explain yourself."

"Daddy, you know how this happened—"

"Nonsense. Clive..."

"Corporate took this account out of our hands, Mr. Hyatt. There's nothing I can do now."

"Of course there is. What's the point of knowing your banker if he can't help you now and again?"

"Daddy." At least EvaMarie had enough spirit to sound disapproving. "Clive has gone out of his way to help us on more than one occasion. We have to face that this is happening."

"Nonsense. I'm not going anywhere." A noise echoed through the room, like a cane banging on the wooden floor, though Mason couldn't see for sure. "Besides, who could buy something so expensive that quick?"

Clive turned sideways, giving Daulton a view of Mason where he stood. "This is Mason Harrington from Tennessee. He and his brother started the purchase proceedings this morning."

"Tennessee?" Daulton squinted in Mason's direction. Mason could feel his pulse pick up speed. "Why would someone from Tennessee want an estate in Kentucky?"

Rolling with that rush of adrenaline, Mason took a few strides into the center of the room. "I'm looking forward to establishing my own racing stables, and the Hyatt estate is perfect for our purposes, in my opinion."

Mason could see the realization of who he was as

it dawned on Daulton's face, followed quickly by a thunderous rage. He was proud to see this glorious, momentous thing that Mason himself had ignited.

"I know you," Daulton growled, leaning forward in his chair despite his wife's delicate hand on his bicep. "You're that good-for-nothing stable boy who put your hands on my daughter."

It was more than just my hands. Maybe he should keep that thought to himself. *See, Kane, I do have control.* "Actually, I am good for something…as a matter of fact, several…million…somethings…" That little bit of emphasis felt oh, so good. "And I'm no longer just a stable boy."

Daulton turned his laser look on his daughter, who stepped back as if to hide. "I told you I would never allow a filthy Harrington in one of my beds. I'll never let that happen."

"Oh, I don't need one of your beds," Mason assured him. "I just bought a nice, expensive one of my own. I'll just take the room it belongs in."

"You aren't getting it from me," Daulton growled.

This time, Mason matched him tone for tone. "You sure about that?"

The other man's eyes widened, showing the whites as he processed that this Harrington wasn't a kid who was gonna meekly take his vitriol. "The likes of you could never handle these stables with success," he bellowed. "You'll fold in a year."

"Maybe. Maybe not. But that will be decided by *me*." Satisfaction built inside as he said it, and he let a grin slip free. "Not you."

He could tell by the red washing over Daulton's face that he got Mason's drift. The older man started to stand. Mason realized he was gripping the side of his chair with an unusually strong grip.

"Daulton," his wife whispered in warning.

But the old man was too stirred up to heed her, if he even heard her in the first place. Mason felt his exultation at besting the monster of his dreams drain to dismay as Daulton took a step forward...then collapsed to the floor.

A cry rang out, maybe from EvaMarie's mom. But everyone rushed forward except Mason, who stood frozen in confusion.

With Clive's help, the women got Daulton turned over and sitting upright, though he was still on the floor. Mason studied the droop of the man's head, even as his back remained turned to Mason.

Kneeling next to her father in dusty sweatpants and a T-shirt, hair thrown up into a messy bun, Eva-Marie still had the look of a society princess when she glanced over at Mason. Her calm demeanor, cultivated through hours of cotillion classes, couldn't have been more sphinxlike. "Could you excuse us for a moment, please?" she said quietly. She didn't plead, but her gaze expected him to do as she asked.

He'd never been able to resist that dark blue, forget-me-not gaze, always so full of suppressed emotions that he wanted to mine.

Then she tilted her head in the direction of the door to the hallway. For once, he didn't have that unbidden urge to challenge that came over him when he was faced with authority. Especially Hyatt authority. Obviously there was more going on here than he was aware of.

Turning, he let himself back out into the hall, wondering if he'd be able to forget the impression that his brother had been right. This wasn't going how he pictured it…at all.

EvaMarie could feel her hands shaking as she finally left behind the drama in the living room to face Mason in the hall. Out of the frying pan and into the fire, as the old saying went. Her body felt like she'd been put in a time machine. All the devastating feelings from that long ago confrontation in the barn—the day her teenage world imploded—had come rushing back the minute her father had raised his voice at Mason.

She'd spent a lot of time throughout her life walking on eggshells, trying not to light her father's fuse. By the time she'd grown a semblance of a backbone, the angry man he'd been had mostly disappeared. He reappeared only during times of high stress, and it was all EvaMarie could do not to give in to her childhood fears.

Now she had to face Mason—with no time for deep breaths or wrapping herself in invisible armor. Just hunkering down, enduring—just like most of her days now. The fact that he was actually here, in this house with her right now, seemed completely surreal, but the derision on his face had been very real.

There had been no doubt in her mind how he felt

about her after all these years. She should take solace in the fact that he hadn't completely forgotten her. But she had a feeling she wasn't gonna feel better about him, or this situation, any time soon.

Maybe a little diplomacy would smooth the way...

"Congratulations, Mason," she said as she approached him with measured steps, trying not to take stock of the new width of his shoulders beneath a fitted navy sports jacket that she never would have pictured him wearing, even if it was paired with a pair of dark jeans and cowboy boots. Talk about surreal...

He turned from his study of the formal dining room to face her, then raised a cool brow. How could he portray arrogance with just that simple movement? "For what?"

"Obviously, you done well to be able to afford—"

"—to no longer be pushed around by people, just because they have more money than me?"

Her entire self went very still. His words told her everything she needed to know—how Mason viewed his childhood, their breakup and her in this moment.

It told her one other thing: he was going to find a lot of satisfaction in this scenario.

Maybe it would be best to focus on business. "So, what can I do for you?" she asked, though she had a feeling he wasn't gonna make it easy...

"That tour I mentioned." He waved his hand in the direction of the stairs. "Lead the way."

EvaMarie simply could not catch a break. She could almost feel his gaze as she took deliberate steps down the rest of the hall, pointing out various rooms.

He wasn't even subtle in his gibes... "Can't say I'm loving what you've done with the place. This version has taken the concept of 'simplify' to a whole new level, I believe."

She couldn't even argue, because she agreed with him. The state of her family home was a drain on her emotional equilibrium every day. But having someone else point it out...well, it certainly hurt.

Should she admit she'd sold off all but her mother's family heirlooms to keep them afloat? Yeah, his reaction to that would be fun. Just one more thing to mock her with.

So she kept silent on that topic, instead launching into a knowledgeable diatribe on the parquet floor pattern, imported tile and other amenities her father had spared no expense on. All the little details she'd spent a lifetime learning that would be useless once she was driven away—but for now she could use them to keep herself from admitting the truth.

She'd done what she could, but the estate was going under, and there wasn't a whole heck of a lot she could do to stop it.

"You're getting a good deal," she said, trying to keep any emotion from her voice.

"A great deal," he conceded.

Color her shocked.

They stood at the top of the back landing, facing a large arch window that gave a clear view to the stables and beyond. It was a mirror of the front of the house, which looked out over the drive and the wooded property between the house and the highway.

Mason studied the view. "Gardener?"

"Um, no," she murmured. "Not anymore."

"That explains a lot," he replied.

Stiffening, she felt herself close off even more. Though she shouldn't be surprised that he just couldn't leave it with the question. From the first words out of his mouth, she had expected his judgment.

"My brother and I would like to offer anyone on staff a job," he said, surprising her. "No need for them to be worried about their incomes because the place has changed hands." He stepped back to the landing, studying the first floor from his higher vantage point. "And we're obviously going to need some help getting things in order."

Yeah, no need for the staff to worry...only her family worried about living on the street... She ignored the implication that the property would need a lot of work to whip it into shape. She'd done the best she could. "That's very generous of you," she said, struggling not to choke on the words and the sentiment. "Currently we only have one employee. Jim handles the stables."

Mason stared at her, wide-eyed. "And the rest?"

"Handled by me."

"Cooking? Cleaning?"

EvaMarie simply stared, not liking where this was headed. Sure enough...

"Well, someone has definitely grown up, haven't they? I can remember days of you being waited on and pampered..."

Unbidden, she flushed. "If that's a backhanded

compliment, thank you." She turned away, breathing through her anger as she stepped over into an open area that branched off into hallways to the various rooms. "The rest of this floor is bedrooms and baths, except for this sitting area."

"Your parents occupy the master suite?" he asked, his voice calm and collected.

Of course it was. After all, he wasn't the one being typecast.

"No. The stairs are too much for my father anymore. There's a set of rooms behind the kitchen. They sleep there." They were originally staff quarters, but she left that unspoken.

"I'll see the master suite, then."

She gave a slow nod, then turned to the short hallway on the left.

"Your father's illness?" he asked, for the first time using a gentle tone she didn't trust at all.

"Multiple sclerosis, though he prefers not to speak of it," she said, keeping her explanation as matter-of-fact as possible. No point in exhibiting the grief and frustration that came with becoming a caretaker for an ill parent. "We've managed as well as we could, but the last two years he's steadily lost his mobility and physical stability."

Her mother had declined also, though hers was from losing the stimulation, social gaiety and status that she had fed off for most of her life.

The grandeur of the master suite swept over Eva-Marie, just as it always did when she entered. It was actually two large rooms, joined into one. Both were lined and lightened by hand-carved, floor-to-ceiling white wooden panels strategically accented in silver-leafing, the same accent that was used throughout the house.

With thick crown molding and a crystal chandelier in each area, the space left an indelible impression. Even empty as it was now.

She stepped fully inside as Mason strolled the cavernous space, his boots announcing his progress on the wood flooring. "There are his-and-hers dressing areas and bathrooms on each end of the suite," she explained. "Though the baths haven't been updated in some time."

"I'm sure we will take care of that," he said, pausing to turn full circle in the middle of the sleeping area. One wall was dominated by an elaborate fireplace that EvaMarie could remember enjoying from her parents' bed as she and her mother savored hot chocolate on snowy days.

She thought of the ivory marble bathtub in her mother's bathroom, deep enough that EvaMarie had been able to swim in it when she was little. It didn't have jets in it like the latest and greatest, but it was a gorgeous piece that would probably be scrapped, if the latest and greatest was what Mason was looking to put in.

Unable to handle any more of memory lane, she turned back toward the door to the hallway.

"And your room?" Mason asked from far too close behind her.

"Still on... On the other side of the floor." She

held her breath, waiting on him to insist on seeing her room. Between them was Chris's room—*please, no more.* She wasn't sure how much longer she could hold herself together.

In an attempt to distract them both, she went on. "The third floor has been empty for years. There're two baths up there. A couple of the bigger rooms have fireplaces. Oh, and the library, of course."

His pause was significant enough to catch her eye.

Did he remember the one time that she'd snuck him in to show him her favorite place in the house? Long ago, she could have spent entire days in the library, only emerging when her mother made her come to the table. Maybe Mason did remember, because he turned away, back to the stairs.

"Another day, perhaps," she murmured.

As they hurried down the stairs, he didn't look back until he reached the side entrance, his hand wrapped around the Swarovski crystal handle.

"If there are any problems, I'll have my lawyer contact you."

She let her head incline just a touch, feeling a deep crack in her tightly held veneer. "I'm sure."

"It was good to see you again." His sly grin told her why it had been—because it had served his purpose.

She wished she could say the same.

Three

"The signing date is set. The property is almost ours." Mason grinned at his brother, then turned back to the lawyer. "You've been great. We really appreciate it."

James Covey grinned back, looking almost as young as them, though Mason knew he was a contemporary of their father. "It's been my pleasure. I'm thrilled to be able to help y'all like this."

His smile dimmed a little, and Mason knew what he was thinking…what they were all thinking. That they wished their father hadn't had to die for this to happen. Kane's hand landed with heavy pressure on Mason's shoulder, and they shared a look.

It wasn't all a bed of roses, but they would honor their father's memory by establishing the best stables money could buy and talent could attain, using everything he'd ever taught them.

It was what he would have wanted.

"So are we going to be running into the Hyatts every time we turn around in this town?" Kane asked as they exited the lawyer's stylish brownstone in the upscale part of downtown that had been renovated several years back. Slowly they made their way down the steps.

Kane had been gone for a week and a half, starting the process of training their new ranch manager to take over their Tennessee stables. They weren't leaving behind their original property, though it wouldn't be their main residence any longer.

"I don't think so," Mason said.

"Good, because that would be awkward."

Mason rather thought he would enjoy rubbing their newfound success in Daulton Hyatt's face, but he preferred not to confirm his own suspicions that he was a bad person. "I'm not even sure what's going on out there," he said. "When I went to tour the stables, no one was there except the guy we're taking on, um, Jim. I haven't seen the Hyatts…or EvaMarie…around town."

"Well, don't look now."

Mason looked in the same direction as his brother, spotting EvaMarie immediately as she strolled up the wide sidewalk headed their way. The smart, sophisticated dress and heeled boots she wore were a definite step up from the sweatpants he'd seen her in, yet he almost got the feeling that she'd put on armor against him.

He wasn't that bad, was he? Okay, maybe he was…

She paused at the bottom of the steep concrete stairs, her dark hair falling away from her shoulders as she looked up at them. "The landlady told me where to find you."

"Um, why were you looking?" Mason asked, ignoring Kane's chuckle under the cover of his palm. He also tried to ignore the way his body perked up with just the sound of her husky voice.

EvaMarie ignored his question and nodded toward the office behind them. "He's good."

"I know." *So there's no getting out of the deal.*

EvaMarie was obviously not daunted by Mason's refusal to relent. She extended her hand in his brother's direction. "You must be Kane?"

His traitor brother went to the bottom of the stairs to shake her hand and properly introduce himself, then he glanced at Mason over his shoulder. "Gotta go. I'll see you back at the town house tonight."

What a wimp! Though Mason knew Kane wasn't running; he was simply leaving Mason to deal with the awkward situation of his own creation. The odds of EvaMarie simply happening by here were quite small, even though the town was only moderately sized with a large population of stable owners in the area.

Sure enough, she waited only long enough for Kane to disappear around the corner before turning back to him. "Could I speak with you, please? There's a café nearby."

A tingling sense told him he was about to be asked

for a favor. Not that the Hyatts deserved one. After all, Daulton had shown no mercy when he'd had Mason's father fired from his job and blacklisted at the other stables in the area. He hadn't cared at all that his father was the sole support of two children. He'd only wanted revenge on Mason for daring to touch his daughter.

Mason would do well to remember that, regardless of how sexy EvaMarie might look all grown up.

The café just down the street was locally owned, with a cool literary ambience that was obviously popular from the crowd gathered inside. Bookshelves lined a couple of walls, containing old books interspersed with teapots and mugs. Tables and ladder-back chairs shared the space with oversize, high-backed chairs covered in leather. He glanced at EvaMarie, only to see her gaze sweeping over the crowd in a kind of anxious scan.

Though he refused to admit it, seeing her do that gave him a little pang. It seemed as though things hadn't changed too much after all. She still couldn't stand to be seen with him in public.

Struggling to stuff down his fifteen-year-old resentments, Mason was a touch short when he snapped, "Grab a table. I'll order the coffee."

"Oh." She glanced his way, her smile tentative. "Could I just get an apple cider please?"

Apparently she hadn't chosen the place for the coffee. As he took his place in line, he couldn't help but think how strange this was. EvaMarie wasn't someone he'd had a typical relationship with—

though she'd been the only woman he'd had more than just sex with. That was a first—and definitely a last.

But they'd never been on a real date, just his graduation party with his high-school friends. Never really out in public. Mostly they had gone on trail rides together, holed up in the old barn loft and talked, sneaking stolen moments here and there when no one was looking.

Once he returned with their drinks, she fiddled with the protective sleeve on the cup, moving it up and down as if she couldn't decide if she wanted to try the drink or not. But she'd requested this meeting, not him, so he waited her out in silence.

Which only made the fidgeting worse. Why did he have to feel such satisfaction over that?

"I found a place for my parents," she finally said. "They'll be moving tomorrow."

"That's nice—is something wrong?"

Just as he'd known it would, his question only made her more nervous. She started to slowly strip the outer layer off the corrugated paper sleeve.

"No," she said, then took a big swallow that was probably still very hot, considering the way she winced. "I'm fine. I just...well, I didn't realize there would be so many people here at this time of day."

"Still embarrassed to be seen with me?" he asked. Then wondered why in the hell those words came out of his mouth.

She must have wondered too, because her eyes

widened, her gaze darting between her drink and his. "No, I mean, that isn't the issue at all."

"Could've fooled me." He wasn't buying it. Especially not with too many bad memories to back up his beliefs.

"And my father's reaction didn't teach you any differently?"

That gave him pause, almost coloring those memories with a new hue. But he refused to accept any excuses, so he shrugged.

"Anyway—" she drew in a deep breath "—they chose to move into a senior living facility so my mother would have help with my dad. The cost of getting them settled is more than I anticipated. I wondered about an extension on the house?"

"Nope."

He caught just a glimpse of frustration before her calm mask slid back into place. "Mason, I can't afford first and last month's rent on a place to live and to pay someone to move all of our stuff."

"Don't you have friends? You know, the old standby—have a nice pizza party and pickup trucks? That's how normal people do it. Oh, right, you aren't familiar with normal people—just the high life."

She looked away. He could swear he saw a flush creep over her cheeks, but he certainly saw her lips tighten. That guilty satisfaction of getting under her skin flowed through him.

She turned back with a tight smile. Boy, she was certainly pushing to keep that classy demeanor, wasn't she? "Honestly, I've spent the last two years taking full-time care of my father. I don't have any—many close friends. And while I'd like to think of myself as capable, even I can't move the bed or couch on my own. I just need—"

He opened his mouth, ready to interrupt with a smart-ass answer, when a woman appeared at Eva-Marie's side.

"Oh, EvaMarie, you simply must introduce me to your handsome friend."

"Must I?"

EvaMarie's disgruntled attitude made him smile and hold out his hand to the smiling blonde. "Mason Harrington."

"Liza Young," she said with a well-manicured hand laid strategically over her chest. "I don't believe I've heard of you—I would most certainly remember."

The woman's overt interest wasn't something Mason was comfortable with—he preferred women more natural than Liza—but rubbing EvaMarie the wrong way was worth encouraging it. Besides, he and his brother were gonna need contacts. Liza's expensive jewelry spoke to money, her confident demeanor to upper class breeding. "I'm new to the area." He glanced across the table so he could see EvaMarie's face. "Or rather, returning after a long absence."

"Oh? And what brings you here?" So far she had completely ignored EvaMarie beside her, but now she cast a quick glance down. "Surely not little Eva-Marie Homebody."

Okay, this wasn't as fun. Mason narrowed his gaze

but kept his smile in place. For some reason, it was perfectly acceptable for him to pick on EvaMarie—after all, Mason justified that he had a reason for his little barbs—but this woman's comment seemed uncalled for.

"The area's rich in racing history," he explained. "My brother and I are setting up our own stables."

"Oh, there's two of you?"

No substance, all flirt. Mason was getting bored. "Lovely to meet you, but if you'll excuse us, we were discussing business."

"Business?" She threw a sideways glance at Eva-Marie, who looked a little surprised herself. "Well, that makes more sense."

Liza giggled, leaning forward in such a way to give Mason a good look into her not-so-modest cleavage. He couldn't help but compare the in-your-face sexuality and lack of subtlety in a woman he had just met with the image of soft womanhood sitting beside her. EvaMarie was smartly dressed, and yes, he detected a hint of cleavage, but she hadn't flashed it in his face in order to get what she wanted. Of course, that thought reminded him of just how much of her cleavage he'd seen…and how much he'd like to see it again. Sort of a compare-and-contrast thing. He remembered her as eager to learn anything he'd been willing to teach her—did she still need a teacher?

Mason quickly reined himself in. There was no point in going there, since he had no plans to revisit that old territory. No matter how tempting it might be. Besides, EvaMarie was looking stoic again. Maybe he should relent—a little.

He stood, then pulled a business card out of his inner jacket pocket. "Well, it was a pleasure to meet you, Liza," he said, handing the card over. "I hope I'll get to see you again soon."

Liza grinned, then reached into the clutch at her side for a pen, wrote on the card and handed it back. "So do I," she said, then flounced back to a table across the floor where several other women were waiting.

EvaMarie had turned to watch her go, then groaned as she caught sight of the other women seated at Liza's table, all of whom were craning their necks to get a good look. "Well, I hope you're ready to announce your presence, because it's gonna be all over town in about two hours."

"That's the plan," Mason murmured. A glance at the card revealed Liza's cell phone number. With a grin because he knew how much it would annoy EvaMarie, he slipped the card back into his pocket. "Now, where were we?"

The pained look that slipped over her face as she opened her mouth, probably to start from the beginning, made him feel like a jerk. So he broke in before she could speak.

"Let me see what I can do," he said. Not a concrete answer, but he needed time to think. And a few more days of worry wouldn't hurt her.

Dang it!

How come Mason Harrington had to show up

every time she looked like a dusty mess? Here she was desperately trying to pack like a madwoman with only five days to move, and he was interrupting with his loud, insistent knocking.

She seriously considered leaving him there on the doorstep, especially since it was raining. Her nerves were strained from the physical labor, emotional stress and learning everything she needed to navigate while losing their home, but a lifetime of training had her opening the door.

But she only forced herself to produce a strained smile. After all, she was exhausted.

"Mason, what can I do for you?"

His lazy smile was way too tempting. "That's not very welcoming."

It wasn't meant to be. And she refused to be lured in by his teasing—a long time ago it had been a sure-fire way to shake her out of a bad mood. Instead of saying what she thought, she simply focused on keeping her smile in place. But she didn't move.

He didn't own the place yet.

"Come on, EvaMarie. Let me in," he added, a playful pleading look to his grin. "I have an offer that will make it worth your while."

She hesitated, then stepped back, because continuing to keep him out was bad manners. That was the only reason. Not that she should care, but a lifetime of parental admonishments kept her in check.

Mason took a good look around the high-ceilinged foyer with its slim crystal chandelier, then walked farther down to peek into a few other rooms on either side.

"Wow. You've made progress." His voice echoed in the now empty spaces.

That's because I'm working my tail off. But again, that was impolite to say, so she held her tongue. She didn't bite it, because she had enough pain right now. Though she'd taken on a large amount of the physical work around the estate, it had not prepared her for all the lifting, dragging and pulling of packing up her childhood home. Her muscles cried out every night for a soak in her mother's deep tub, but even that didn't relieve the now constant ache in her arms, thighs and back. Definitely hard on her back but great for weight loss.

He glanced down the hallway toward the back of the house. "Is your father here?"

She shook her head. "Why? Worried?"

"Nope." Again with the cute grin, which was making her suspicious. Why was he being so nice? "Just didn't figure it was good for him to get all riled up."

For some reason, she felt the need to defend her parent, even though Mason was right. "He hardly ever does anymore. Not like he used to. He had a heart episode about six years back that forcibly taught him the consequences of not controlling his temper." She gave him a saccharine smile. "I guess you're just special." Or inspired a special kind of hatred maybe.

"Always have been," he said. If he'd caught the insult, he let it roll off him.

His nonchalant handling of everything she said made her even angrier. Luckily, she was used to holding her emotions deep inside.

"Actually, I finished moving them to an assisted living facility yesterday."

Mason's raised eyebrow prompted her to explain. "I chose to put them there because at least I'll know there's someone to look out for them. Even though I feel that someone should be me." The place had cost a small fortune, but she was hoping being out from under the crippling mortgage payments would help. Now, what did she do about herself? Well, she hadn't figured that out yet.

Hopefully she'd find something soon, or she might just break down in a panic attack. She hadn't been kidding when she said the first and last month's rental deposits put most places out of her range. The fact that she didn't even have friends she could call on to let her sleep on their couch made her feel lost and alone.

"Do you work?" Mason asked.

The change in conversation came from out of the blue. "What?"

"A job. Do you have one?"

His tone implied she didn't even know what one was. She certainly wasn't going to tell him about the new career she was building. He would probably think she was crazy or arrogant to believe she could make a living off her unique voice.

"Taking care of my parents and this place was my job," she answered, even though most people didn't view it that way. Mason probably wouldn't either, even though it had been damn harder than a lot of things she could have done. And asking one of the families they knew in the area for a job would have meant exposing her parents' failure to their world. She'd chosen not to go against their wishes.

True to form, Mason asked, "How'd that work out for you?"

"I did the best I could," she said through gritted teeth.

"Think you could do better with a better boss and actual resources?"

Now she was really confused. "What?"

He turned away, once again inspecting the rooms. "My brother and I have plans—big plans. To establish our stables is a simple matter of quality stock, training and talent." He turned back, giving her a glimpse of his passion for this project. Guess buying this estate wasn't only about revenge.

"Establishing a reputation—that's a whole different story," he said, his gaze narrowing, "and we don't have the breeding to back it up."

She knew all too well how hard it was to keep and make contacts within society here—after all, her father had kept his illness a secret in order to protect his own social reputation. It took two things to break into the inner circle around here: breeding and money. Preferably both. But they'd accept just the money if someone was filthy rich.

"We can fast-track it—after all, money makes a big first impression."

A surreal feeling swept through EvaMarie. Honestly, she couldn't imagine she was talking to the same boy who'd held her so long ago. Sure, he'd talked horses and racing. She'd known he'd wanted to own his own stables one day—but money had never come up. Then.

They'd both been naïve to think it hadn't mattered.

"Which means we will be turning this into a showplace," Mason said, sweeping his hand to indicate the room.

"What does that have to do with me?"

He cocked his head to the side, a lock of his thick hair falling over his forehead. "You've lived here all your life?"

She nodded, afraid to speak. His sudden attention made her feel like a wild animal being lowered into a trap.

"I bet you know this place better than anyone."

"The house and the land," she said, feeling a pang of sadness she forced herself to ignore.

"So you could come to work for me. Help with the renovations. Prepare for the launch. I'll even give you more time to move everything."

Her heart started to pound as she studied him. "Why?" Revenge? Everything in her was saying to run. Why else could he possibly want this?

"I need a housekeeper. I'm assuming you need a job," Mason said with a nonchalant shrug. "You need time to figure this all out. That's what you were asking for, right?"

Regardless, working with him every day? Watching him take over her only home and never being able to show her true emotions for fear he would use them as a weapon against her? The last few encounters had been experience enough. *No, thank you.*

She shook her head. "I don't think that's a good idea."

"You don't?" He stepped closer. "Seems to me you're about to be out of a home, income... What's the matter? Afraid your friends will find out you have to get your hands dirty for money?"

That was the least of her worries. Her parents had feared that—yes—but not her.

He moved even closer, giving her a quick whiff of a spicy aftershave. Why was he doing that? Suddenly she couldn't breathe.

"I'll give you a job and a place to live. Sounds a whole lot better than the alternative, don't you think? And in return I get someone who can make this renovation move even faster."

Looking into his bright blue eyes, she wasn't so sure she agreed. There had to be a catch in there somewhere...but she truly wasn't in a position to turn him down.

Four

EvaMarie smoothed down her hair, wishing she could calm her insides just as easily when she heard Mason come through the side door. From the sound of other voices, he wasn't alone.

This time she was prepared.

Or so she thought. First she caught sight of Mason's brother, Kane, who had filled out just as much as his brother. The two men were like solid bookends; carbon copies with broad shoulders and muscles everywhere. If only Mason's shoulders were available for resting on. How incredible would it feel to have someone to rely on for a change? To lean against his back, feel his bare skin against hers, run her fingers down along those pecs—

Whoops. Not the direction she should let her mind

wander down right now. Especially as the three men before her all turned their attention her way. The middle one—slighter than the brothers—looked vaguely familiar.

Kane stepped forward, intimidating in his size and intensity, until a smile split his serious look. "Hello, EvaMarie. I'm Kane."

"I remember," she murmured, and shook his hand. What a surprise. No smart remarks. No ultimatums. Looked like at least one brother could be reasonable. "Mason didn't say when you'd be joining us." She could sure use a buffer from his brother.

"Oh, I won't be moving in right away. I'm still tying up some loose ends at our base camp, and we invested in a town house when we were scoping out the landscape." He shared a glance with his brother. "But I'll be here soon enough."

The thought of being here alone with Mason set off a firestorm of nerves inside her.

"After I get the chance to work my magic on this place. I've been waiting years," the slender man said as he moved forward. He didn't have the bulk of the other two, but she could tell he made up for it with loads of personality. The good kind.

"Hello, EvaMarie," he said, holding out his hand. "It's been years since we've seen each other, so I don't expect you to remember me. I'm Jeremy Blankenship."

"Oh, yes. I thought you looked familiar. It's good to see you again…"

Now that she had a name to go with the face, her

memories clicked. Jeremy was a son of one of the active horse racing families who had decided to go completely against the grain and attend school for an interior design degree.

"Can we move past the pleasantries and get to work, please?" Mason groused.

"You'd better get used to pleasantries and small talk if you plan on socializing much in this town," Kane warned.

Jeremy nodded his agreement before turning his gaze back to EvaMarie with questions in his soft brown eyes that had her tensing. "When I heard the Harringtons had bought the estate, I didn't expect to find you still here."

Before she could answer, Mason cut in. "Eva-Marie will be overseeing a lot of the daily work and details for me."

Jeremy looked between them for a moment. "Oh, so are y'all together?"

"No." Mason's voice was short, but EvaMarie wondered if that was a hint of satisfaction she heard. "When I say she'll be working, I mean it literally. As in, for me."

There it was... EvaMarie felt her face flame, blood rushing to the surface as she wondered how many other people he would find satisfaction in telling her new status to. Part of her wanted to crawl away in defeat, but she forced her shoulders back, projecting a confidence she was far from feeling. With any luck, this job would be a gateway to a new life for her. One that wasn't going to be at the same level as she'd had growing up, but despite what a lot of people were probably gonna think, she was fine with that.

At least she'd be one step closer to this life being *hers*.

There was no point pouting over what she couldn't change…yet. That was one thing life had taught her. The key was to simply put her head down and power through. "Jeremy, would you like a look around?" she asked, assuming that's why he was here.

"Would love it. After all, I can't interior design if I haven't seen the interior, right?" He smiled big, as if to show her his approval, then linked his arm through hers and led her down the hallway.

She might just like having him here.

Most of the rooms were just going to need new wall treatments, updated lighting and furniture. Uncomfortable at first, EvaMarie soon put forth a few tentative ideas and received an accepting reaction from all but Mason, who remained aloof though not outwardly antagonistic. She directed the little party around the downstairs, then into the kitchen and family room.

"This would be a great place for a leather sofa and big screen television," Kane said. "Right next to the kitchen. Perfect hang out space."

The discussion devolved into name brands and types of electronic equipment that had EvaMarie yawning. Then Kane climbed the three steps to the main kitchen area. The rest of them followed. EvaMarie tried not to cringe. This room had been in desperate need of a makeover for years. Its mustard yellow appliances and farm motif dated it from the early eighties at the latest.

"I want more extensive work in here," Kane said. "Stainless-steel appliances, new granite countertops, the whole shebang."

"My brother," Mason interrupted, "in this area, I give you free rein."

"That's because you don't want to starve," Kane teased.

Mason winked, pointing at his brother. "You are correct, sir."

Without thought, EvaMarie said, "Well, looks like one of you learned to cook."

The men glanced her way. Once more she felt that telltale heat in her cheeks. Maybe she'd gotten a little too comfortable—the last thing she should have alluded to was her one and only trip to the Harrington household when she was a teenager. That's when she'd realized that the extent of Mason's cooking skills included opening a box and the microwave door. Of course, hers weren't comprehensive, but her mother had the housekeeper teach her the basics. She'd enjoyed it so much she'd taken home ec and some specialty classes once adulthood allowed her to pursue a small number of her own interests.

"Well, we will definitely coordinate these two spaces so they flow together," Jeremy said, smoothly glossing over her sudden embarrassed silence. He gestured back toward the living area beyond the bar that served as a divider between the two spaces. "Do you gentlemen want a true man cave here or something more subtle?"

"Man, too bad there isn't a place for a big game room," Mason said. "We can at least watch the Super Bowl on a big screen here, but something more intense would be a great addition."

Kane nodded. "Pinball machines, a poker table, a wine cellar. Wouldn't that be awesome?"

"What are the odds of us getting something that's awesome?" Mason asked Jeremy with a grin.

"Well, all of these first-floor rooms are open to the hallway. How true to the style of the house do you want to hold to?"

The guys bantered back and forth, Mason's smile breaking through full throttle. For the first time, EvaMarie caught a true glimpse of the Mason she remembered. Oh, he was older, more ruggedly handsome. But that smile showcased the fun-loving, friendly resonance of his youth.

She'd missed it, as much as the thought scared her.

As they talked more and more about what would make a really cool splash in the house, EvaMarie could feel her stomachache growing. Ideas sparked in her brain...as did the voice of her father calling her a traitor. The push and pull of what should be clear family loyalties confused her. After all, her family had had a difficult time with what life had thrown at them. While losing their home was just part of that life, losing it to the Harringtons was unforgivable to her father.

She shouldn't be helping them. But she needed to do a good job, right?

"What about the basement?" she asked, the words bursting forth before she'd actually made up her mind.

The three men shared a glance, then Jeremy asked, "What basement?"

EvaMarie offered the interior designer a tentative smile despite her guilt and led the way back out to the breezeway. On the far side of the stairwell was a regular door that opened to a fairly wide set of stairs. She could feel Kane as he leaned around the doorway. "Looks promising," he said.

"What it's gonna look is dusty," she said as she started down, flicking the light switch on as she went. "I can't even remember the last time anyone was down here."

She'd actually forgotten about the space, which was currently used for storage. Probably a good thing. Thinking about packing and moving all the stuff down here too might have thrown her over the edge of what sanity she had left.

Funny the things you could block out to protect your mind in a precarious state, she thought.

"Wow. This is incredible," Jeremy was saying as his dress shoes clicked on the concrete floor.

"The open space runs under this half of the house," EvaMarie explained, relaxing a little in the face of his enthusiasm. "Since the house was built into the hill, they finished this portion for the square footage. But with only the three of us, there wasn't any need for it."

As Mason's expression darkened, she decided it was time to keep her mouth shut again. The men explored, brainstorming all the cool things they would do down here, sparing no expense on Mexican tile and glass block room dividers and yes, a place for pinball machines. Her input was no longer needed. Not wanting to get in the way, EvaMarie wandered back the other way to the one room on the other side of the stairway. A large open entryway framed the room beyond like a picture.

The long-mirrored wall reflected the ballet bar attached at a child's level. She could also see her elaborate doll house closed up in the corner. The few stuffed animals she'd kept were resting safely in the wooden toy chest. This had been her own space when she was a little girl—a safe haven from her father's unreasonably high expectations and her mother's silent pressure to conform.

A safe haven, until her mother had created the library on the third floor the year she turned twelve. It had been her birthday present.

"Havin' fun?"

Mason's voice right behind her head caused her to jump. Her heart thudded, even though there wasn't any danger. Was there?

She glanced over her shoulder to meet his gaze. "Sure."

"Just don't have too much fun. You're here to work, remember?"

I don't think you'll let me forget, will you? Probably not the most appropriate response to an employer...

Kane paused on his way to the stairs to pat Mason's shoulder. EvaMarie could hear Jeremy's shoes on the steps as he ascended.

"This is gonna be great," Kane said with a grin before he headed up.

EvaMarie had marveled at the camaraderie between the brothers. After all, she hadn't had a sibling in a long time. Certainly not as an adult. Would Chris have stood by her through thick and thin? He'd been extremely protective of her, so she had a feeling he would have.

Only he'd never gotten the chance.

"You're lucky. It's wonderful that you have a brother like that," she said, her gaze trained on the stairs though her eyes remained unfocused, wishing for something she couldn't have.

"Actually, it's wonderful to have someone at your back when the world turns on you."

The sharp tone penetrated her thoughts, the pain catching her attention. She glanced Mason's way to find his glare trained on her, close and uncomfortable.

"Yes," she whispered. "Yes, it is."

As if he knew he'd made his point, Mason walked away, leaving EvaMarie with the uncomfortable knowledge that she'd reminded him exactly why he was here...and why she was here too.

For a few minutes she'd forgotten, and that could be detrimental in a lot of ways.

Then he glanced over his shoulder to deliver another dictum. "The furniture for my bedroom will be here tomorrow. You'll set it up good for me, right?"

Sure. She had no problem performing what should be a perfectly normal task. So why did it feel so intimate to her?

A few very rough days later, EvaMarie bent from the waist and let her upper body hang toward the ground in an attempt to stretch her aching back. Since the work in the basement was scheduled to start simultaneously with the upstairs renovations, she had a week to get it completely emptied.

Which wasn't nearly long enough to handle the relics from two generations—all by herself. Regardless, she still had to be ready for the moving team in two days.

Faintly she heard something through the sound of her own exertions and the radio she'd turned on to help keep her mind off how lonely this job was. Standing up straight, she cocked her head to the side, trying to get her bearings as the blood rushed down from her brain. *Was that footsteps?*

Crossing the room, she cut off the radio just in time to hear her name coming from the direction of the stairs.

Great. Just what she needed—Mr. High-and-Mighty, probably showing up to give her just one more task to demean her pride and heritage. He'd been unbearable these last few days.

Even though it irked her no end, sometimes she

could almost understand. Being at someone else's mercy wasn't fun. And knowing that person could control the fate of your entire family? Definitely scary. Mason must have been so angry and petrified when he'd left here as a teenage boy.

But the constant interruptions and subtle—or not so subtle—digs as he demanded she clean out the garbage disposal, bag up and carry out trash, and clean his toilet, all while he watched with a smug expression had worn out her patience long ago. Hell, her father wasn't even this obnoxious.

She hadn't realized when she agreed to take this job that she'd be serving as his whipping boy.

"I'm in here," she called as she heard him walk past her childhood playroom.

He stopped in the doorway with a hard step, back tight, frown firmly in place. "Why didn't you answer me?" he demanded.

"I didn't hear you."

"What do you expect when you shut yourself away down here with a radio on? Anyone could have waltzed right on in and made themselves at home."

She studied him for a minute, trying to figure out where this irritating attitude had come from. "You told me to come down here and clean it out so Jeremy could get work started," she said, keeping her voice calm but unable to control lifting an eyebrow. "That's what I'm doing."

"Part of working for me is being available."

Okay, she'd had about enough. "To do what? Kiss your feet?"

"What?" he asked, his head cocking to the side.

"Look, this high-and-mighty attitude is getting old—"

"You don't like the new me?"

*Not really...*if he just weren't so darn sexy.

"Ah, can't say anything nice, huh?"

If you can't say anything nice, don't say anything at all. How many times had her mother admonished her with those words? "It's just unnecessary. I know you hate my guts, but wouldn't it be more pleasant to be civil?"

"No," he said with a grin that was just as smug as it was sexy. "I'm enjoying this just fine."

"I'm sure you are."

He took a few steps closer, managing to appear menacing even though the grin never left his face. "If you have a problem with me, you're welcome to leave. I'll even give you a day to get all of your stuff, and your family's stuff, out."

Right. She just stared, feeling her mask of self-preservation fall into place. She'd let him see way too much of herself by arguing with him. It accomplished nothing other than giving him more ammunition for pushing her buttons.

"What can I do for you then, *boss*?"

Mason smirked. He knew he had her right where he wanted her. "Come with me. You're gonna love this."

Probably not, but what choice did she have just yet? Soon though. Soon she'd have enough savings and steady work in her new career lined up to make it on her own. Until then, she simply needed to keep her head down and endure.

Of course, it didn't stop her exhausted mind from questioning what task he had in store for her now—and whether her already taxed body was up to snuff for it.

The worry didn't set in good until they'd already traversed the length of the upstairs hallway. Then she followed him out the side door and across the parking area in front of the four-car garage. They passed the gleaming pickup truck he drove and her own much older sensible sedan. Then he turned onto the path to the stables.

This couldn't be good.

EvaMarie had taken on a lot of physical labor since her daddy had gotten sick, but one thing she'd never done was the heavy lifting in the stables. Feed the horses or brush and ride them—sure. But that was the extent of it.

Plus, she'd already worked all morning packing in the basement. And the day before that, and the day before that...

Mason finally paused beside the stall where Eva-Marie's mare Lucy resided. The satisfaction marking his face told her his anticipation was high. Too bad it was all at her expense.

No matter what, she wouldn't cry in front of him.

"We're bringing in our best mare later today from the home farm. Kane should be here this evening. I'll be back in three hours to make sure this stall is cleaned and ready for her."

EvaMarie studied him for a minute. Surely he was joking, pulling a mean prank. "But Jim's not here."

"You are." His expression said he wasn't budging.

Stand up for yourself. Automatically, her stomach clenched, nerves going alert just as they had her entire life. Taking a stand did not come naturally to EvaMarie. Her daddy had squashed that tendency when she was knee high to a grasshopper. "I don't do stables."

"Says who? Is that written down somewhere that I missed?"

Her jaw clenched, but she forced the words out anyway. "You know it's not."

"Welcome to the world of manual labor." He skirted back around her, heading for the barn door. Even the sight of that high, tight butt in fitted jeans didn't lift her mood. "Have it done in three hours," he called over his shoulder.

"I can't!"

Mason turned back with a frown. "Princess, employees shouldn't try to get out of work. It doesn't look good on their evaluations."

"But I'm already working. In the house."

"Good. Then you won't mind getting dirty."

Five

This was gonna be so much fun...

Mason eyed the man in the dark suit who stood near the side door to the house, staring at it as if he could divine who was inside through the exalted abilities of his birthright alone. The tight clench of Mason's gut and surge of anticipation told him that his body remembered this man well...and the role he'd played in the destruction of Mason's family all those years ago.

He hadn't actually seen Laurence Weston since he and Kane had returned to town, but Mason had hoped he would have the chance to rub the snitch's nose in his success at some point.

He just hadn't planned on doing it here at the Hyatt estate.

"May I help you?" Mason's words were polite. His tone...not so much.

Laurence turned to face him with an expectant expression that reminded Mason of his own youthful expectation of having everything go his own way. Laurence had felt the same, only exponentially, and he'd made it a point to let those "beneath" him know their purpose was to serve—and not much else.

"I'm looking for EvaMarie."

"Right." Mason turned for the stables, leaving Laurence to follow if he wanted.

At least, Mason assumed she'd still be out here. Was she capable of cleaning out a stall in three hours? A month ago, Mason would have answered with an emphatic "no," but he grudgingly admitted that EvaMarie had changed a lot since he'd last seen her. Other than knowing how to saddle a horse, the teenage girl he'd fallen hard for wouldn't have known how to work the business end of a shovel, or pitchfork, or rake... Though he hadn't been there to see the actual work, the adult EvaMarie had made some impressive headway inside the house this week, without any help that he could tell.

Which just irritated him even more. Why was she working so hard, staying so loyal to a family who had obviously taken her hard work and obedience for granted? Which led him to do stupid things like put her to work in the barn...

A glance into the stall showed that she was indeed capable of cleaning one in a few hours. The straw bedding and buckets were fresh and clean. There wasn't even a hint of manure in the aisle for Laurence to step in, darn it—Mason would have loved to see those Italian loafers ruined.

Petty, he knew. Just like giving the princess the job of cleaning the stables. But this man—when he'd been a boy—had deliberately told EvaMarie's father where to find them together, simply because he'd wanted EvaMarie for himself. Considering they weren't married now, it must not have worked out the way Laurence had planned.

As they moved farther into the cool, dim depths of the stables, Mason heard the low hum of a husky voice. His entire body stood up to take notice. Man, that siren voice had played along every nerve he had when they were dating, lighting him up better than any drug. Sometimes just talking to EvaMarie on the phone was as good as seeing her in person. Now he felt the same physical charge—no other woman's voice had ever affected him like that.

More's the pity.

She'd grown into its depth though. As she came into view talking to one of the mares in a stall farther down, he compared the wealth of hair piled on her head and strong, curvy body to the delicacy she'd possessed as a young woman. His daddy had said she wouldn't stand up to one good birthing.

Then.

Now she was a strong woman capable of handling what life dished up to her—*so why was he piling on the manure?*

Before he could do something stupid like voice

his thoughts, EvaMarie glanced up, spying him over the horse's back. Her features expressed the weight of her exhaustion, emphasized by the dirt smudging her cheeks and the pieces of hay sticking out at odd angles from her hair. But her words were as polite as always. "The stall is ready."

Which was what he'd wanted, right? He'd set out to demonstrate the hard work he'd done for her father once upon a time. Teaching her a lesson was his aim in keeping her here, wasn't it?

So why didn't seeing her like this, exhausted and dirty, make him happy?

"Why the hell are you cleaning stalls?"

As Laurence's voice exploded in his ear, EvaMarie looked to Mason's left with wide eyes. "Laurence?" she asked.

The other man stepped around Mason and got a good look at EvaMarie's disheveled state. "What is going on, EvaMarie? You don't answer the phone. You don't show up for this week's committee meeting. And now this?"

Mason could feel the hairs on the back of his neck lift, hackles rising as another male attempted to assert himself in Mason's territory. And he wasn't at Laurence's mercy like he'd been as a kid.

"Shouldn't you be asking me that?" Mason said, stepping around to take a stand between Laurence and the stall door. "After all, I'm the boss around here."

Laurence's incredulous glance between the two of them almost made Mason laugh. Obviously this was something he couldn't comprehend. Finally Laurence asked, "And who are you, exactly?"

Mason wanted to smirk so badly. In fact, it may have slipped out before he caught it. "I'm Mason Harrington."

It took a minute for the name to register. After all, what need would Laurence have had for that nugget of information all these years? Then his eyes widened, his gaze cataloging the adult Mason. "And you're the boss, how?"

Behind him, Mason heard the stall door open, but he wasn't about to let EvaMarie deprive him of the joy of putting Laurence in his place. "I'm the new owner of the Hyatt Estate."

Laurence trained his hard gaze on EvaMarie. "How is that even possible?"

The rich never wanted to believe that one of their own could fall...unless the fall worked to their advantage somehow.

"The estate went into foreclosure, Laurence," EvaMarie said in a hushed tone. "We were forced to sell."

Mason braced his legs, arms crossing firmly over his chest. "And I simply couldn't wait to buy."

"Wasn't your dad just a jockey? A trainer of some kind?"

If anything, Mason's spine stiffened even more. "He was a one-of-a-kind trainer whose career you ruined with your little disclosure to EvaMarie's father all those years ago."

Laurence's gaze narrowed, but Mason wasn't about to let him get away without hearing the facts.

"But it didn't matter in the end. Upon his death, my father left Kane and I enough money to buy this estate and start our own stables. Probably five times over." He took a step closer, edging the other man back. "We may have been easy targets back then, but threatening us now would be an unwise move…for anyone."

Laurence stood his ground for a minute more, though Mason was close enough to see the staggering effect his current situation had on Laurence. "How is that even possible?" he asked.

"I know it's hard to imagine someone bettering their circumstances through hard work—" and a lot of deprivation "—but the truth is, I earned it."

I earned it.

Those words rang in EvaMarie's ears as she ushered Laurence back toward his Lincoln. Mason was right—he'd always worked hard. Since she'd been working for them, it had become very obvious he and Kane had no plans to rest on their laurels and simply enjoy their money.

She couldn't help comparing Mason to Laurence, who had gone to a good school thanks to his daddy's money, coasted by and gotten a job in his daddy's real-estate business where he sold off of his personality when he actually tried, and let someone else handle the paperwork for minimum wage.

She wasn't immune to his faults, but he was the one friend who had stuck with her all this time, despite knowing some of the realities of the Hyatts' situation. He was also the only one her parents had let see what was really happening to them. Even though they were holding out hope she'd eventually give in and marry him, this was the one area of her life where she'd built a wall of resistance.

"How could you let this happen, EvaMarie?" Laurence asked, digging his expensive heels into the driveway to bring them to a halt. "All you had to do was call me. I could make all of this go away. Easily."

Only if she accepted his conditions. In that, he and Mason were very similar—every offer came with strings. Why Laurence was so insistent that he wanted her, she couldn't fathom. With his uninspired track record when it came to work, he should have given up long ago.

"I told you I can handle myself."

"By losing the family estate? Great job."

That stung.

"Why didn't you call me?" he went on. "Tell me you were in this much trouble?"

"It was my dad's decision whether or not to share. You know how careful he is. He didn't want word to get around."

Laurence shook his head, hands on his hips. "He's not gonna be able to hide it for long with those yahoos horning in."

That sounded like sour grapes to EvaMarie. "Regardless," she said, "I'm simply staying until everything is up to standards. By then, my plans will allow me to support myself."

"Plans to do what? Work yourself to death?" He grabbed her forearm. "Spend your days dirty?" He used his hold to give her a good shake. Her irritation shot through the roof. Laurence's voice rose to match. "Where do I stand in those plans?"

EvaMarie felt her backbone snap straight despite her fatigue. "Don't. Start."

His grip tightened, as if he was afraid she'd escape. He crowded in close, giving her an uncomfortable view of his frustration. Memories of several such confrontations with her father caused her stomach to knot.

"You know I can give you the life you deserve," Laurence insisted, his breath hot on her face. "Pampered and taken care of instead of cleaning up after your parents and that guy." His expression tightened with disgust as he assessed her with a sharp glance. "I mean, look at you."

Yes, look at me.

For a moment, just a brief moment, she was tempted to stop fighting and let someone handle life for her for a change. Tears of exhaustion pushed their way to the fore.

"It's what our parents always wanted," Laurence said, his voice deepening. It was low and husky in a way that left her cold. It shouldn't...but it did. But he was insisting... "We'd be perfect together."

Until the thrill of getting what he wanted wore off. Through years of dealing with Laurence, EvaMarie had learned he was like a big child who wanted a toy to entertain him and an adult to handle all the hard stuff. After the goal was accomplished, EvaMarie would simply be left taking care of Laurence, just as she did everyone else, and be expected to make his life as easy as possible.

Hers would be just as hard. Just as lonely. But he didn't see it that way.

"Everything okay?"

EvaMarie glanced to the side and saw Mason eyeing Laurence's hand on her arm.

Laurence glared, refusing to budge. "Yes," he insisted.

Ever the diplomat, EvaMarie reached up to pat his hand with hers, wincing at the unexpected pain in her palms. "Everything's fine," she agreed. Then she gave Laurence a hard look. "Goodbye, Laurence. I'll see you at the library committee meeting next week."

He looked ready to protest, but then adopted a petulant expression and let go of her arm. Because it was easier. Because in the end, he was still an overgrown child.

Which was evidenced by his defiant gunning of his engine on the way out. EvaMarie rubbed her arm, once again feeling that sharp pain in her palm. She glanced down, but one quick peek at the red, raw patches on her skin had her hiding her hands by her sides.

"Seriously?" Mason asked. "That guy is still around?"

EvaMarie tried to hide the exhaustion that was now starting to weigh her down like a heavy blanket. She just wanted a shower and her bed. If she didn't get inside soon, the shower wasn't happening. "Laurence is a friend of the family."

"But not part of the family? Bet that's a disappointment to your father."

He had no idea. The only thing her father continued to badger her about these days was Laurence. Though he wouldn't say it explicitly, Daulton saw Laurence as the answer to all of his problems. No matter where that left EvaMarie.

Too tired for more politeness, she headed for the door. Mason could follow or not. "There's a great many things I do that are a deep disappointment to my father," she mumbled.

Her choices had always been wrong—ever since her brother had died. The smiling, applauding father had long ago turned into the disapproving dictator. Illness and age had quieted him, but not mellowed him. "Anyway, Laurence is just looking out for me."

"Don't you mean looking out for his investment?"

She skidded to a stop on the tile in the foyer. "What?"

"Well, he's put a lot of years into pursuing you. Wouldn't want all of that effort to go to waste."

"Effort isn't even a word in his vocabulary." If Mason thought any different, he didn't know Laurence at all.

But she might have underestimated Mason. He quirked a brow as he said, "Ah, I see you've gotten to know him quite well. Took you a while."

No, she'd always known how Laurence was. Only no one had trusted her to make the right choices, only the easy ones. They'd expected her to give in to her parents' demands and marry the man they wanted for her. She might have given up a lot in her lifetime, but that choice was not one she was willing to let go of. She did have boundaries, even if no one else bothered to see them.

Or respect them.

Wearily she made her way up the stairs, her feet feeling like lead weights. If only she could pull on the banister for support, but she had a feeling her hands wouldn't appreciate the pressure. "Good night, Mason."

"Wait. Why are you stopping for the night?"

Because I can. She didn't answer at first, just kept on going with all the energy left inside her.

When she reached the landing, she finally repeated, "Good night, Mason," and dragged herself to her room.

That man was like arguing with a brick wall.

Six

Mason winced as he bumped into the banister in the dark, then wondered why on earth he didn't turn on the lights before he fell down the back staircase.

Nightlights were placed at intervals along the hallway, but didn't help him with the unfamiliar spaces and shadows. Lightning from the thunderstorm beating the house from outside lit up the nearby arched window, giving him a chance to locate the light switch. The hanging chandelier lent its glow upstairs and down, allowing him to make better progress on the stairs and in the hallway.

As he approached the family room, he heard a noise. Looked like it was time for a little midnight tête-à-tête with his roomie.

As he made his way through the darkened family

room into the kitchen, with only a faint light burning above the stove, the muffled sounds he'd heard morphed into husky curse words that were creative enough to raise his brows. Apparently the princess had gotten herself an education while he'd been gone.

This should be interesting.

Flicking on the overhead lights, the first thing he noticed was legs. Bare legs.

EvaMarie stood next to the bar in a nightgown that barely reached midthigh. Beside her were open packages and what looked like trash strewed across the counter. She blinked at him in surprise…or maybe it was just the bright lights.

Mason stepped closer. "Problem?" he asked, unable to keep the amusement from his voice.

If she'd been a kid caught with her hand in the candy jar, she couldn't have turned redder. Her body straightened; her hands slid behind her back.

"Nope. Everything's fine."

Right. Her shifting gaze said she had a problem, just one she didn't want him to know about.

He stalked to her, even though he knew being close to all that bare skin wasn't the best idea he'd ever had. But seeing the first-aid kit in the midst of all the wrappers, he realized this wasn't the time to play.

"All right. Let's see it," he said, his tone no nonsense. "After all, we don't have time for you to be off duty."

Those dark blue eyes, so thickly lashed, couldn't hide the wash of tears that filled them. Alarm slammed through his chest. He could handle a lot of things, power through just about every situation. But put him in the vicinity of a woman's tears, and he was hopeless.

Luckily she blinked them back, but then murmured, "It'll be fine." Her lashes fell and skimmed the flushed apples of her cheeks. "I'll be fine by morning. Just go back to bed."

Even Mason wasn't that self-centered. Gentling his voice, he said, "Just let me have a look, Evie. Okay?"

Her eyes connected with his. He saw his own surprise reflected there. He hadn't called her that name in too many years. But it worked, because her hands slipped from behind her back, as though she instinctively trusted that connection.

For once, he refused to use it against her. She didn't need that right now.

Or ever, his conscience chastised him.

Pushing his conscience aside to deal with later, he cupped her hands in his and turned them over so he could see the palms. "Holy smokes, EvaMarie. Why didn't you wear gloves?"

He could feel her stiffen and try to pull back. Her fingers curled as if to protect the wounds from his judgment. "I did," she insisted. "The only pairs I could find were all too big. They kept slipping against my skin."

Alarm mixed with a darker emotion, deepening his voice. "I can see that. Looks almost like you have carpet burn on your palms. Let me have a better look."

As he led her over to the stove so he could get some direct light, she said, "I cleaned them as best I could in the shower, but the soap burned—"

"I bet."

"My wounds weren't that dirty. The gloves kept the dirt out for the most part. But I think they need to be wrapped." She glanced over her shoulder at the mess on the bar. "Only it's kind of hard to do one-handed."

And it hadn't occurred to her that there was now someone else in the house she could ask to help her. Why should it? His conscience flared up again. He'd proved pretty well so far that his job was to make her life harder, not better.

He cradled one of her hands in both of his, bending closer for a good look. Memories of holding her hand abounded, but he couldn't remember if he'd ever examined her there in this much detail. He was pretty sure those calluses on her palms and fingertips hadn't been there before. The skin along the back still felt silky smooth and smelled faintly of lilacs. Was that still her favorite scent?

And when he noticed the faint outline of curvy, muscled legs down below the bar, his body went a little haywire. The mix of past and present was throwing him off balance.

For a moment, he could almost understand her father's protective nature, the desire to shelter her from harsh reality—though Mason could never forgive the lengths her father had gone to achieve that aim. No one deserved to have their life ruined like that, not Mason, not his father.

As he surveyed the abraded skin, the damage done by his own selfishness, a strange compassion kicked in. One he almost resisted, almost ignored. Man, it sucked to realize his brother had been right. They'd been joking with each other, but Mason *had* done a bad thing.

"Let's get these wrapped up so they don't get dirty. I think they'll heal in a few days, but we don't want infection getting in where the skin is broken." He turned back to the bar, breaking their physical connection. The cool air he drew into his lungs cleared his head. The sound of the rain outside ignited thoughts of starting over.

As long as he didn't let himself get too close, get drawn into the attraction that flirted behind the edges of his resentment. Therein lay the real danger he needed to protect himself from.

"Then how about I make some hot chocolate?" he asked, remembering it as her favorite drink. "That'll warm us up before trying to sleep."

"So you have learned to cook?" she asked, cautious surprise lightening her voice.

"No, but I make a mean microwave version."

EvaMarie held herself perfectly still.

Her insides jumped and shivered with every touch of Mason's fingers against hers, but she refused to let it show. Part of her wanted to relax into his newfound compassion. After all, she remembered an all-too-nice version of Mason that she wished would come back.

But the bigger part of her couldn't forget his behavior since his return. Better not to trust that this version would last longer than it took to feed her hot chocolate and send her to bed like a child.

Maybe that was the key—treating her like a child. After all, he didn't seem to care for the grown-up version of her too much.

His touch was amazingly gentle as he applied a thin coating of antibacterial ointment to each palm, then set about wrapping her hands in gauze and tape. Memories of other times he was gentle, like the night she offered him her virginity, pushed against the barriers she had erected to block them out of her brain. What good would it do to relive those times? After all, he hated her now. Thinking about it would get her nothing but grief.

But she'd pulled out the memories of their loving often over the years. Mason had been her first, and best, lover. Her one experiment in college to replace those memories had proved a disappointment. So her time with Mason was all she had to live on during the long, lonely nights of her adulthood. But she had learned one lesson from that lackluster experience in college: settling for something less than what she'd experienced with Mason wasn't worth the trouble.

Which had kept her from making several stupid choices that would have easily gotten her out of this house years ago. Like marrying the man who had pestered her to do so since she'd turned eighteen.

EvaMarie's suspicions grew as Mason deposited her at the nearby table, cleaned up all the wrappers and discarded bandages, then went to search in the pantry. Some food had been delivered on the same day as his furnishings and personal items, but she didn't remember any hot chocolate mix. But sure enough, he pulled out a round brown canister with gold lettering: a specialty chocolate mix, her one indulgence.

The awkward silence in the room, broken only by the sounds of Mason and the rain outside, urged her to do the polite thing and speak. But what subject wouldn't be fraught with unexploded land mines? As she studied the expert wrapping on her hands, she knew she had to try.

"So I suspect that your purchase of the estate is the talk of the town, or will be soon," she said, her voice hushed in deference to the night and the storm outside. For some reason it just seemed appropriate, even if a touch too intimate. "It's really incredible, Mason. I'm proud of you and Kane for being so successful."

And she was. Her one visit to the Harrington farm when they were dating had shown her just how different their lifestyles were. Mason's family hadn't lived in poverty, but their situation had probably been what EvaMarie now knew as living paycheck to paycheck. Mason's dad had cooked her a simple meal of homemade fried chicken, and macaroni and cheese from a box. It had been good, and the atmosphere around the table had been friendly and welcoming.

Mason hadn't been able to understand when she said it was the most comforting night of her life. He hadn't understood what life was really like for her… and she hadn't wanted him to know the truth.

"I know your dad must be too," she added.

Mason turned away from her as the microwave dinged. "Actually, my father's dead."

"Oh, Mason. I'm so sorry."

He was silent for a moment before he asked, his voice tight, "Are you?"

"Yes. He seemed like a nice man."

"He was. He didn't deserve the lot he had in life. Constantly undermined and unjustly ridiculed by people who didn't even know him, but who had all the power."

The spoon Mason used to stir the hot chocolate clanked against the side of the cup with a touch more force than necessary. EvaMarie winced, knowing that he was talking about her father, and his father's former employers. She held her breath, awaiting a return of the snarky, condescending man he'd shown her since his return. Instead, he crossed the kitchen and set the mug before her without comment.

She wasn't sure how to respond, so she remained quiet. The steam from the cup drew her. She wrapped her aching hands around the outside, letting the heat slip over her palms into the joints, then up her arms. So soothing… "So he left you an inheritance?" she asked, hoping to steer him away from the touchy subject.

"Actually, it was my mother."

EvaMarie nodded, though she'd never heard much about the woman before. Lifting the cup close, she breathed in the rich chocolate scent. The comforting familiarity cloaked her in the very place where familiarity seemed to have gone out the window. This was her kitchen, the one she'd drunk hot chocolate in all her life, but it wasn't hers anymore. And the man next to her wasn't hers either.

"We moved back to Tennessee where she was from, though my grandparents on her side wouldn't have anything to do with us for the longest time. My grandfather never did come around."

"Why?" She couldn't get out more than a whisper and found herself grasping the mug just a little tighter.

"They were high society, lots of money." His glance her way said *sound familiar?* "They never approved of the marriage, or the fact that their daughter died after he took her away."

The level of Mason's resentment after all these years was starting to make a little more sense. "They wouldn't come see her?"

Mason shook his head, his hands clenching where they lay on the table. "My father even sent a letter after receiving her diagnosis. He knew it was bad. My grandmother later told him her husband refused to allow her to open it. They didn't see her before she died."

A stone-like weight formed in EvaMarie's chest. "How awful."

"My mother had a sizable trust fund created for us. Over time, my father managed to grow it out of proportion to what she left us. But he never touched it."

Considering how much they had struggled after his father lost his job, EvaMarie couldn't imagine that kind of sacrifice. But she daren't mention it for fear it would make Mason angry again. This small moment of civil conversation was a gift she didn't want to squander.

"He told us about it after his first heart attack. Helped us decide what to do and taught us how to manage it. It was—" he paused, shaking his head "—*is* still amazing to me."

"That's an incredible gift," she said.

"Yes. And he was an incredible man."

Indeed. To have taken such care with his wife's gift for her sons, even when it made his own life harder than it had to be—that was a true father. EvaMarie struggled not to make a comparison to her own father, to the lack of foresight he'd exercised, but her heart remained heavy.

As she sipped, the downpour outside quieted to a light, steady rain, soothing instead of boisterous. The ache in her palms had subsided some beneath the warmth and care of her bandages. And Mason had surprised her. They hadn't talked, truly talked, in many years. She shouldn't be enjoying it this much.

Her eyelids drooped. The day had been a long,

hard one. And she'd start an even busier one tomorrow on even less sleep. As much as she wanted to savor this truce while it lasted, it was time she headed back to bed.

Standing, she glanced across at Mason, only to catch him surveying her bare legs. Almost as quickly he looked up, but she pretended not to notice. "Um, I think it's time I headed back upstairs," she said. Then trying to smooth over the awkwardness, she asked, "Is your room set up all right?"

"Yes, thank you, EvaMarie."

She tried to squash the glow that blossomed at his words, but couldn't. Tomorrow, he'd kill the glow soon enough.

"Well, good night. Thank you for the hot chocolate and, well…" She nodded toward her hands.

Mason stood, as well. "It's the least I can do, EvaMarie."

She took a few steps back, then paused. "Until tomorrow." She turned and made quick progress toward the hall. She'd almost made it when she heard him behind her.

"EvaMarie."

Heart pounding, though she knew it shouldn't, she glanced back. "Yes?"

"You have a storage building already, correct?"

And just like that, they were back to boss and employee. Why did tears feel close all of a sudden? "Yes. I promise all arrangements have been made and the moving guys will be here on Wednesday to have everything out in time for the renovations to start."

He stepped closer, looking mysterious as the darkness hid his expression. "Actually, a moving crew will be here tomorrow to help you. All you have to do is direct."

The bottom dropped out of her stomach like she'd taken a fast-moving elevator. "What?"

He didn't move, didn't speak for a moment. Then he let out a deep sigh...one she'd almost mistake for regret. "Just consider it hazard pay."

Seven

"I'll be on the second floor if you guys need me for anything, okay?" EvaMarie said.

"No problem. Thanks, Miss Hyatt."

With a deep breath, EvaMarie headed up the stairs from the basement, skirting the carpenters already measuring for their plans to widen the entryway. Sad to say, but she'd rather be down there helping with the packing, even with her sore palms. But she had another job waiting for her.

With the extra help, her family's belongings were going into storage a lot quicker than she'd anticipated. Which meant she had to get her brother Chris's room cleaned out ASAP. She was surprised Mason hadn't asked about the other empty room on this floor, but she was grateful. She didn't want movers in there.

Yet cleaning it out herself wasn't a task she was looking forward to.

Her hand trembled as she reached for the doorknob. As if this wasn't gonna be hard enough.

"Is this where you'd like the boxes, Miss Hyatt?"

EvaMarie almost jumped, but caught herself before turning back to the young man. "Yes, please." After he set them and some tape down in a neat pile, she added, "Thank you so much for bringing those upstairs."

"No problem."

His gaze flicked to the still-closed door before he turned back toward the stairs. He might be curious, but he wasn't going inside. No one had been inside that room except her and her mother for over twenty years. Not even her father.

Turning back, she took a deep breath and forced herself through the door. A quick glance told her everything was the same. A small part of her had wondered if her mother would take something from the room with her when she left, but it didn't look like she had.

In fact, the room remained exactly as it had been when Chris had died in a tragic car accident here on Hyatt land. He'd been fifteen. The emotions of that day stood out so vividly in EvaMarie's mind, though the actual images were mere shadows now. She'd been angry with her brother because it was one of those rare times he'd refused to let her tag along on his adventure. It was one of the few times he'd disobeyed their father. He wasn't supposed to be in the vehicle unsupervised.

While he was out, he'd lost control of the truck, and it plunged headfirst into a ravine. His chest had been crushed against the steering wheel. By the time anyone found him, he was gone from her forever.

But his room remained full of old-school video games and a huge television, the best model from that time. Horses were everywhere, whether it was pictures or his collection of carved wooden figures. While Chris had been a typical teenage boy, he'd loved the family's animals and looked forward to taking over from their father someday.

A Tennessee football bedspread and pillowcases. A BB gun and his very first rifle on the gun rack above the bookcase. Even a pair of discarded cowboy boots peeking out of the barely open closet door. How did she even begin to pack away the life of someone she loved and missed so much—even to this day?

She picked up the photo box she'd brought in the other day, along with some trunks to pack away the more valuable keepsakes, and walked over to the wall beside the bed. Pictures of Chris at various sporting events and horse shows, some of him alone, some with her or their parents, were barely hanging onto the wall. The tape had deteriorated over time. One by one she took them down, removed what adhesive was left and packed them away in the box. Her mom might not want them now, but eventually she might. EvaMarie had long ago made secret copies of the originals for the scrapbook she kept in her room.

"Whatchya doing?"

Whirling, EvaMarie tilted off balance before righting herself for a good look at Mason. "Oh, I thought you were gone for the day."

He shrugged, but his gaze steadily cataloged the room around them. Her hands tightened on the box until the edges cut into her bandaged palms. She didn't hide her wince soon enough.

"I took care of some stuff in town," he finally said. "Then I came back to see how things were going. Looks like they are making steady progress in the basement."

Her voice was breathless as she tried to justify herself. "Yes, I planned to get back down there—"

Again that nonchalant shrug. "You did fine. They were very clear on what you wanted done. You've gotten everything pretty organized."

"I try," she murmured. It felt weird to acknowledge the compliment, as if she needed to search for some hidden insult. After last night, she wasn't sure what to expect.

Or quite how to react.

"How're the hands?"

"Better." She gestured with the box. "Awkward."

"I'm sure. Let me know when you need some new bandages."

Which just reminded her of the two of them in a dimly lit kitchen and how she had been half-dressed. That had been an ill-timed choice, but when your hands were on fire and you needed to get to the first-aid kit, putting on pants moved low on the priority list. At least he hadn't seemed to mind...

A flush swept up her body and bloomed in her cheeks. She nodded and turned away, anxious to hide her reaction.

Behind her, she heard him moving, prowling the space. She bit her lip. Though she knew the reaction was unfounded, part of her ached to stop him. Her mother wasn't here to care that there was a stranger in Chris's room, but it still felt wrong.

"Can I ask whose room this is?"

Despite his gentle tone, despite last night, she was still afraid to say. Afraid of the condemnation or judgment that might come from the revelation. But it wasn't as though she could hide it with him standing right behind her.

Gathering the last of the pictures into the box, she carefully put the lid on top and laid it on the desk near the door. "This room belonged to my brother, Chris."

Mason's slow nod didn't give her a clue as to his thoughts. "You've never mentioned him before."

No, she hadn't. Not even when she and Mason had been close. So his accusing tone was justified—this time.

How did she begin to explain that it was a barrier her parents had put up that she was almost afraid to cross? Especially since her own grief, never properly expressed, might have broken through the dam if a crack had ever appeared. Even now, she wasn't sure what openly experiencing her grief would have been like.

"My parents—" she cleared her throat, trying to loosen the constriction "—they never talked about him."

He shook his head. "How is that even possible? Not to talk about your own child?"

Now it was her turn to shrug, because she didn't understand it as well as she wished she did. Even now, she couldn't explain her tight throat or pounding heart. It made no logical sense, but the sensations were there, nonetheless.

Still, she forced herself to speak. "Once we came home from the funeral, he wasn't ever talked about again. Everything about him disappeared, except this room," she said, glancing around with a covetous look. "As if he didn't exist—at least, it felt that way."

She stroked a finger down a picture of Chris on his favorite horse that sat framed atop the desk. "Only I know that wasn't true. At least, not for my mom."

"How?"

She pursed her lips before she spoke. "Because mine is the next room over. I could hear her crying in here some nights." She took a shuddering breath, remembering the eerie, sad sounds. "But no one mentioned it in the morning."

Behind her, she could hear him moving but was too caught up in her emotions to turn around.

He asked, "So you were old enough to know him, to remember it?"

EvaMarie turned around and nodded. "He was

quite a bit older than me, but the age gap didn't keep us apart. Chris took me everywhere with him. Taught me to ride horses, swim. We were rarely apart. He was my champion." Her voice trailed to a whisper. "My protector."

He'd protected her from their father and his demands for perfection, even at her young age. After Chris's death, her father had become her jailer. For a long time, she'd understood the need to keep his only living child safe. Until Mason. Until she'd become desperate to finally live.

"I don't remember hearing about his death, but then I'm only a couple of years older than you."

"It was sudden, a car accident here on the estate. When something isn't talked about by the family, and no one dares ask, it becomes a matter of out of sight, out of mind."

A few steps brought him closer, almost to within arm's length. EvaMarie was amazed at how desperately she wanted him to close that distance, to hold her against him until the sad memories dissolved.

"But why would *you* never tell me?"

Her gaze snapped up to meet his. Unnerved by the intensity of his stare, she swallowed. For a moment, she considered giving some kind of flippant, casual answer. But something about that intensity demanded a true reason.

So she gave it. "You'd be amazed, I'm sure, at how deeply a family's darkest moments can be buried. When something makes you happy, the last thing you want to do is remember the bad times."

Which was why she'd never been completely honest with him about her father, even. Yes, she'd warned him they needed to be careful. That she wasn't allowed to date. That her father would probably run Mason over with his truck if he caught them together—if he didn't get his gun first. But she'd never told him that her father scared her. That he controlled every last second of her life, demanding that she be the perfect, compliant child.

Because she didn't want to taint their time together with the darkness she lived with every day.

Her chest tightened, threatening to cut off her air supply. Time to change the subject. "Thank you, Mason."

"For what?" he asked with a slight tilt of his head.

"For listening, letting me talk about him." The words were rushed, but if she didn't get them out quick, they wouldn't come at all. "Though I wish I'd had more years with him, I try to remember how he lived while he was with me."

His slight smile told her he could relate. "My father always said, the least we could do to honor my mother was to keep her alive through our memories, to keep her a part of our family. He talked about her until the day he died."

"I wish we had." EvaMarie's heart ached as she looked over her brother's possessions. "I'm so out of the habit now...it feels weird." She lifted her head. "And it shouldn't."

And somehow, she'd find a way to change this...

just like she was changing a whole lot of other things in her life. So with a deep breath, she got started packing.

Mason followed his brother into Brenner's, breathing in the smell of grilled meats and a real wood-burning fire. This wasn't a touristy place but had a huge local following—off the beaten path.

Though they had a varied menu, their steaks and Kentucky microbrewed beers were a superb version of man food.

Kane stretched in the booth, taking in the roaring fire nearby and the authentic aged brick walls. "Can you believe we're here and eating at a place like this?"

"As opposed to the cheap burgers that were a treat growing up?" Mason shook his head. "Kinda hard to believe, even now. But dad would have loved this."

Mason thought of the man who had worked so hard, taught them so much, and had still laughed and had a beer with them... He shifted, uncomfortable comparisons with what he now knew of EvaMarie's childhood rising up in this mind. But before he could mention anything to Kane, the waitress appeared.

By the time their orders went in and their foam-topped beers had come out, Mason thought better of sharing. After all, it really wasn't his story to share. Since EvaMarie would be working with Kane some too, he didn't want her to be uncomfortable if Kane let his knowledge slip.

While he and his brother both sat in thoughtful

silence, Mason couldn't help but think about the changes in their circumstances that were so unexpected, so welcome, and yet made him long for the man who had made it all possible. Their lives could have been very different if their father had been a different kind of man.

As if on the same wavelength, Kane raised his mug. "To the man who sacrificed so we could have all this."

They tapped beers and drank. The smooth amber liquid had just enough bite for Mason's satisfaction. "Dad loved us," he said. "That much is clear."

"Was always clear," Kane agreed.

Again Mason came back to EvaMarie, her childhood, her family. He'd had something she'd never had for all her privilege: the unconditional love of a parent.

Kane went on, "I'd like to think he'll be happy with us naming the stables after him. He was so excited when we told him what we wanted to do."

But not about them moving back here. The one and only time Mason had mentioned that idea, his father had become visibly upset. Maybe through the years he'd realized just how hard the persecution had been on Mason, and had probably known that if he got within a hundred miles of the Hyatt family, revenge would be the only thing on his mind.

"You okay, Mason?" his brother asked.

Suddenly he realized he'd been staring into his drink. But the last thing they needed right now was his confused thoughts on the Hyatts complicating their vision for their racing stables. "Yeah," he said. "Harringtons. Quite an upscale ring to it, I'd say."

They shared a grin before Mason raised his glass once more. "We'll make it everything he would have wanted." If he could have had what he wanted in life…or rather taken their money to build what he'd wanted. "He was a selfless man, you know," Mason said, preaching to the choir. "Makes me wonder if I can even attempt to live up to the man he was."

Kane raised a brow in query at the sudden turn of the conversation. "Living in the same house with EvaMarie got you thinking a little differently?"

"How'd you guess?" Mason hated a know-it-all.

"Brother, there's a reason I opted to oversee the transition at the home farm when we decided to buy the Hyatt estate. You need time to work through things, good or bad."

"I didn't expect it to be good. Didn't expect…" *Her.* He shook his head. "This isn't going how I planned."

"Told ya so."

Mason had a suspicion his brother was making fun of him. Now the smirk made it obvious. "I'm glad you're enjoying this."

"Then we're both happy."

"Smart-ass."

"And practical." Kane winked. "EvaMarie seems like a nice, capable, intelligent woman. How can she possibly complicate your life that much?"

"You'd be surprised," Mason mumbled.

"Then I guess you shouldn't have hired her then, huh?"

Mason hated it when his brother had a point. Luckily the waitress brought their food just then, filling the table with enough plates of steaks and sides and bread to keep them busy for quite a while. Then she headed back for another round of beer.

Mason was savoring his first bite of succulent meat when Kane's grunt drew his attention. Kane's gaze followed the activity over Mason's shoulder.

A quick glance and Mason wanted to grunt himself. Daulton and Bev Hyatt were making slow progress across the main part of the restaurant floor, patiently accompanied by the friendly hostess who was chatting with the one and only Laurence Weston. Mason's very own kryptonite, all at one table.

He turned back to his food. "Well, that's great."

And it only got worse. The hostess was making for a table not too far away. In fact, it was directly across the fireplace from the booth Mason and Kane occupied. Right on the edge of Mason's peripheral vision.

So much for enjoying dinner.

He pushed back, wiping his mouth with a few rough strokes of his cloth napkin. "I'm done."

"Admitting defeat already?" Kane asked with an arched brow.

Why did his brother have to be such a voice of wisdom? "Are you thirty-two or eighty-two?"

Kane shrugged, that trademark Harrington grin making another appearance. "Not my fault someone has to be the adult."

He wasn't joking, no matter what that smile said. Only two years Mason's senior, somehow Kane always played the adult role. He wasn't prone to the same emotional outbursts as Mason. Very few people had seen his serious side—and they definitely regretted it when they did. When crossed, snarky, joking Kane turned cold and calculating.

A scary thing to see, even for Mason.

So he acknowledged his brother's point with a short nod and returned to his food. No reason why the other family had to impact his and Kane's dinner, which had started on such a bright note.

The brothers' conversation turned desultory before they regained their normal rhythm. Their refreshed beers helped.

But it wasn't long before the weight of unwanted attention settled on Mason. He considered ignoring it, but he just wasn't that kind of person. A casual glance to his right showed him that, sure enough, the Hyatts were staring. Laurence had his gaze trained almost defiantly on the couple, as if he refused to lower himself to looking Mason's way.

Mason dipped his chin in a single nod of acknowledgment, then returned his attention to Kane. "Was that adult enough?" he asked, hoping to lighten the mood.

Kane grinned. "Sure."

But apparently it wasn't enough for Daulton. Within minutes, snippets of the conversation across the fireplace struck them like pellets from a BB gun.

"—just a shame, in this day and age, people like that can come in and steal everything you've worked for."

The low rumble of other voices answered. Mason met Kane's look across their table. His brother sighed. "This is going to be interesting."

Mason tried to ignore it. He really did. But Daulton Hyatt had no compunction about slandering the Harringtons in a public restaurant. At all.

"In my opinion, there's a reason God lets people be born with no money. Everyone has a station in life. That's an indicator. And a predictor of future behavior."

The bright flush radiating from Bev Hyatt's cheeks was almost painful to see, but Mason noticed she never made an attempt to quiet her husband. She simply worried the edges of the cloth napkin beside her plate. Laurence's remarks must have been more moderate in tone, since Mason couldn't make out the words, but whatever he said seemed to spur Daulton along.

"Those Harringtons don't even know what to do with a horse, much less a stable of them," he said loudly enough to turn a few heads from the tables around him. "You mark my words," he said, adding emphasis by shaking his steak knife, "they'll be a complete failure within a year."

Kane was on his feet two seconds quicker than Mason expected. He followed, eager to provide backup.

"I'm not sure I heard you correctly," Kane said. "Did you mean we'd be as much of a failure as you were?"

The older man straightened, obviously unused to being challenged. "I am not a failure."

"Really?" Kane wasn't backing down...and he chose not to lower his voice either. "Because your stables were in bankruptcy when we bought it. Was that from mismanagement? Lack of knowledge? Or sheer laziness?"

Oh boy. Kane was dangerously calm as he went on. "You mark *my* words, old man. We aren't afraid to fight dirty, so I'd pull my punches if I were you."

Daulton Hyatt turned to his companions. "Listen to how they talk to me. Guess their father was as inept a parent as he was a businessman."

Mason quickly sidestepped to force his body between Kane and the table. Otherwise, Mr. Hyatt would have been counting his broken teeth. Unconsciously, he reached for his own form of ammunition.

"That's a strange attitude for you to have, considering your daughter is working for me now," Mason said with a deadly quiet reserve that he knew wouldn't last for long. Unlike Kane, he enjoyed yelling.

He could see the surprise knock Daulton back a little, but he never looked away. Bev glanced across at Laurence with wide eyes. Whatever she saw there made her swallow hard.

"My daughter would never betray me by working for you," Daulton blustered. "She got a job at the library."

"Sure about that?"

Daulton must not have liked what he saw in Mason's eyes. "EvaMarie is a good girl. Too good for the likes of you. Or did you somehow trick her into doing this like you tricked us out of our house?"

Now it was Kane's turn to restrain his brother. His hand on Mason's arm was the only thing that kept Mason from slamming his palms on the Hyatts' dinner table. "You know, EvaMarie is a good person, a good *woman*."

His emphasis on the last word did not sit well with EvaMarie's parents. Their eyes widened, full of questions. Questions that Mason would never stoop to answering.

"It's amazing that she's turned out as well as she has," he went on, "considering the overbearing, manipulative father she's put up with all her life."

"Overbearing? Dear boy, that's the last thing I am." Daulton's chest puffed out. "I made sure my child learned right from wrong, how to be a true lady and how to conduct herself with respect. Which is more than your father ever taught you."

Kane's deliberate removal of his hand from his brother's arm signaled exactly how hard that blow hit. But this time, Mason used words instead of fists. He leaned onto the table, getting close to Daulton's face even though he didn't lower his voice. "My father was more of a man than you'll ever be. He cared for his family instead of browbeating them." He shook his head, driven to break through the man's steely facade. "He would never have completely erased a son from his life simply because he had the gall to die on him."

"Mason!"

Jerking around, Mason found himself facing EvaMarie. The flush of her cheeks and slight sob to her breath told him if she hadn't heard everything, she'd heard more than enough. But it was the accusation in her eyes, the betrayal in that look that cut past his defenses.

For once, it was more than deserved.

Eight

"How could you disgrace us by working for that man?"

The Harringtons were barely out the exit before the interrogation started. A quick glance around at their fellow diners only reinforced EvaMarie's wish that her father would lower his voice. After all, she was only across the table from him.

With few other options, she modeled a lower tone. "That man and the job he offered me—a great paying job along with room and board—are helping us get through our…situation," she insisted.

"I don't see how," Daulton said, leaning back in his chair and crossing his arms over his chest. It was a stubborn pose if ever she saw one. A pose she'd seen him adopt often in her lifetime.

She knew, just looking at her father, that Mason's outburst wasn't his fault alone. Her father could provoke the calmest of people. And right now, her own anger was rising hot. Anger at Mason. Anger at her father. It was threatening to crackle the paint off her inner walls, walls that had locked away years' worth of emotions and kept her calm and collected for far too long.

She leaned forward, crowding over the table. "*You* can't afford to live in that facility, Dad. I know you'd rather not face it, but that's the reality." Her heavy sigh might seem mild to most people, but was a risky move with her father. "When are you gonna face how life really is, Dad—for you and for me?"

As her father's expression closed off even more, her mother joined the conversation for once. "But to tell Mason those things—personal things about us…"

Sadness and guilt mingled within EvaMarie as she watched her mother clutch her cardigan together at the vulnerable hollow of her throat. Compassion softened her response. "I'm sorry, Mother. Mason found me clearing out—" she choked slightly, still unable to speak her brother's name in front of them "—the room. I gave an explanation. It never occurred to me—"

"That he'd use it as ammunition?" her father interjected. "How naïve are you, EvaMarie? That's the kind of man he is."

Laurence nodded. As much as EvaMarie wanted to argue that Mason wasn't like that, that she'd seen him laugh with and support his family, show compassion even to her when he probably didn't feel like she deserved it, she'd heard his accusation herself.

"How could you lie to us, darling?" her mother asked. "We thought you were working at the library?"

"Shocked me too," Laurence added.

With a quick sideways glance, EvaMarie mumbled, "You aren't helping."

But Laurence wasn't backing down. He loved stirring the pot. "Honey, you weren't born to clean barn stalls."

The surround sound gasps told her he'd gotten his point across. That was the problem with Laurence... always had been. He was only willing to further his own agenda.

"No daughter of mine—" her father started.

The smack of her palm on the table sounded impossibly loud to EvaMarie. No one else in the restaurant even looked in their direction, but she felt like she suddenly had a 1000 kilowatt light shining right on her.

It was always that way when she dared defy her father.

"Yes, I will." She enunciated clearly, hoping she could get her point across in one try. The quiver in her stomach told her the chances were iffy, but at least a numbness was starting to creep over her raw emotions, giving her a touch of distance as she delivered what was most likely her long-needed declaration of independence.

"I will do whatever I'm told by Mason. I'm not a princess, not anymore—face it, Dad. I'm a worker bee."

The breath she drew in was shaky, fragile. "This is my life. One I am struggling to resurrect out of the gutter after years of trying to keep us afloat. What did you think would happen when you left me to clean up the mess you left behind? I'm doing the best I can with what I have to work with here."

Shocked silence was a new response from her parents. A novel one, in fact. Thank goodness, because she wasn't sure she'd have been able to withstand any dictums to sit down and shut up. Instead EvaMarie stood, palms firm on the table to keep her steady. "I thought you'd be proud of me, Daddy. After all, you're the one who taught me not to argue with authority."

The reality of what she'd said didn't honestly hit EvaMarie until she was on her way home. Then she had to pull the car over until she could get her shaking limbs under control. How could she have talked to her parents like that? But then again, every word had been honest.

Though her father regularly wielded his honesty like a sword, EvaMarie had never been allowed to own hers.

Her emotions were in turmoil, overflowing until she didn't know how to contain them. Especially when she ran into Mason on the upstairs landing. Suddenly she had a target for her deepest emotion: anger.

"How dare you," she demanded, stomping across the landing to crowd into his space.

He straightened, withdrawing only an inch before staring down at her intently. EvaMarie felt her emotions go from hot to supernova.

"Your dad was deliberately pushing my buttons," Mason said, for once the calm one in the situation. "You should have heard what he said before you got there."

She shook her head, her mind a jumble of thoughts and questions, but one stood out from the rest. "Why would you talk to him in the first place?"

His incredulous look didn't help matters. "How could I not? He made sure he spoke loud enough for the whole restaurant to hear."

Well, that did sound like her father. "That's no excuse."

"Actually, it's enough of an excuse. I'm not gonna sit by and let him malign my family and keep my mouth shut."

"But it's okay to retaliate by throwing his dead son in his face?" She stomped closer, close enough to feel Mason's body heat. "I trusted you with that information—something I've never done with another living soul. Why would you turn around and tell it to anyone? Much less use it as a weapon against my father?"

"I got angry," he said with a shrug. "Kinda like you are right now, only you're much cuter."

EvaMarie wasn't sure what happened. One minute they were facing off. The next the knuckles on her right hand burned and Mason gripped his left arm. She'd…oh man, she'd hit him. Her whole body flushed.

When Mason pushed forward, she instantly retreated. Standing her ground wasn't something she'd ever been good at, especially when she was afraid. If he decided to retaliate, she certainly deserved it.

Then her back met the wall. His body boxed her in. She looked up into his face, fear gripping her stomach, only to have his lips cover hers.

This wasn't a teenage kiss. It was rough, powerful, and had EvaMarie's body lighting up all on its own. Leaving anger far behind, she wanted nothing more than to drown in the hot rush of need that overtook her in that moment.

Suddenly his teeth nipped the sensitive fullness of her mouth. Her gasp gave him free access. He pressed in, those vaguely familiar lips giving her a good taste of what he was capable of as an adult. This was no innocent exploring. Instead he conquered. With every brush of those lips, every stroke of his tongue, her body bowed into his without compunction.

Without thought, she pressed her palms against his sides, her fingers digging into his rib cage to urge him closer. Images of his body covering hers forced tiny mewling sounds from her throat. How had she lived this long without having him again?

Suddenly he pulled back. Bracing his hands over her head on the wall, he rested his forehead against hers. The sound of their rapid breathing was loud in her ears. *No, please don't leave.*

She should be embarrassed by her need, ashamed to want a man who had set out to make her life miserable. But she couldn't find the self-preservation to care. It was hidden somewhere beneath the desire that had lain dormant in her body for fifteen years— and was now clamoring for fulfillment.

Then his hand pressed up on her chin, forcing her to face him. By sheer will, forcing her to open her eyes and see the man behind the touch.

"I know I'm a safe outlet for your anger, Eva-Marie. Much safer than your family," he said, still struggling to get his own breath under control. That gave her more than a hint of satisfaction. As did the deep timbre of promise that resonated in his words.

"But remember, that doesn't mean I won't retaliate."

Mason awoke the next morning with the taste of EvaMarie on his lips and the scent of her in his head.

Still.

That fresh taste of guilelessness with a dark undertone of desire was like rich chocolate, igniting Mason's hunger for more. But there was too much history. Too many complications.

Yeah, he just needed to keep telling himself that— no matter how many times his body reminded him just how soft she'd felt, how much fuller she was as a woman, with intriguing curves that he ached to spend a night exploring.

Nope. Not gonna happen.

Grabbing a pair of jeans, Mason dressed quickly

and headed downstairs. He could hear the faint sound of workmen from the basement. But there was no EvaMarie in the dining room, family room or kitchen, and no fresh coffee either. He made quick work of getting it set to brew, and stared broodingly out the window.

He shouldn't want to see her, but here he was searching around every corner. What was his problem?

Jeremy called to him from the hall. "Morning, Mason. Hope we didn't wake you."

"Nope. That basement has great soundproofing."

His friend grinned. "Good thing, considering the sound system you guys want installed."

"Oh yeah." That was gonna be fun.

Jeremy nodded toward the hallway. "Wanna take a look at the wall treatment going in the formal dining room? It's about halfway done."

"Sure." Mason paused long enough to fill a coffee mug, then followed. "When are the new floors going down?"

"Two weeks."

He grinned. "I'll make sure I'm absent that week."

"I don't blame you," Jeremy said, then presented the room under construction with a hand flourish worthy of Vanna White.

After admiring all the improvements Jeremy had gotten done in a very short amount of time, Mason finally got down to what he really wanted to know. "Have you seen EvaMarie this morning?"

Jeremy nodded. "Sure. She was in the barn when

we got here this morning. She came over to let us in, then she went back." A frown marred his young face. "Looked like she'd had a rough night. You haven't been making her clean out more stalls, have you?"

Mason paused, eyeing his friend over the rim of his coffee mug. "Told you about that, did she?"

Jeremy eyed him back. "That was not nice."

And Mason wouldn't be allowed to forget it. "I know. Of course it won't happen again."

Jeremy looked skeptical but let his line of questioning dry up.

As soon as he could escape, Mason dragged on his boots and headed for the barn. Jim's truck was in the drive, which made EvaMarie's presence in the stables that much more of a mystery.

As he stepped into the cool darkness of the large building, he heard the faint murmur of EvaMarie's voice. Just like the other day, all his senses stood up and took notice. The farther he walked, the clearer the words became until he realized she was singing a lullaby. As he walked past Ruby's stall, the mare had her head out of the box, ears pricked forward as she stared down the aisle toward the source of the soothing tones. Apparently Mason wasn't the only one entranced.

The sound originated from the double stall down on the far left. As he reached the half-door, Mason couldn't see EvaMarie's upper body because the mare had crowded over the half-door to her stall to rest against EvaMarie's shoulder as she sang. He could see a delicate hand resting on the horse's neck, the flash of blunt-cut nails as she lightly scratched in time with her song.

An ache shot through him, so strong his knees went weak.

Swallowing hard, Mason watched that hand—so graceful yet so capable—until the horse pulled back to glance into the stall behind her.

Jeremy had been right—EvaMarie was a mess. He'd go so far as to say she looked worse than when she'd cleaned the stall. Almost as if she'd slept all night on the barn floor.

"Yes," she crooned at the animal, unaware of his observance. "You have a pretty, pretty baby."

"That she does," Jim said, appearing from the other side of the stall door. "Very pretty indeed."

A baby. The mare had foaled during the night... which explained a lot about EvaMarie's appearance. Jim grinned when he saw Mason standing there.

"She delivered about two hours ago," he said, bringing EvaMarie's attention his way. Mason wanted to grin as she suddenly smoothed a hand over her hair, then plucked out a piece of straw, but figured she might not appreciate that he found her disheveled state cute.

"Why didn't you come get me?" he asked instead. "I could have helped."

"She's not your horse," EvaMarie replied, quiet but firm. "Besides, Lucy did the work. We were just here in case of trouble."

The reserve he heard in her voice was clear. Mason just wasn't sure if she was still angry with him, or embarrassed by their confrontation the night before. He couldn't resist teasing her to find out.

"Sure looks like you worked hard to me...all night long." He let that grin slip out. "Jeremy accused me of making you clean out stalls again."

Her cheeks flushed pink. He would swear he heard her mumble as she turned away, "You'd think they'd never seen a woman get dirty before..."

Oh, Mason hadn't...at least not in the way he wanted.

Funny how EvaMarie could do the simplest of things and it would crack his resistance like a sledgehammer—like laugh with Jeremy, blow across a cup of hot chocolate, bristle at Mason's comments. Every move was way sexier than it should be—or maybe he just had a really dirty mind.

As she disappeared from his range of sight, Jim inched closer. "She told me about the argument with her father."

"Yes?"

Jim didn't look angry, so maybe Mason wasn't in too much trouble.

"Well, there's lots of time to talk while you're waiting and watching for a birth to happen. Anyway, Mr. Hyatt has always been a difficult man. I almost quit more than once."

"Been here long?" Mason didn't remember the older man from his brief stint here as a teenager.

Jim nodded. "I was here for a while, then moved to Florida for several years to care for my wife's parents. We moved back after they both passed away."

Mason knew he shouldn't ask, didn't have the right to, but he heard himself asking anyway. "Were you here when Chris died?"

"Yes," Jim said, his tone low as he glanced toward the stable entrance as if seeing something that wasn't there. "I watched Mr. Hyatt carry that boy's body out of the woods himself. It was a tough time for everyone, but especially for EvaMarie."

"Losing a brother must have been hard, especially at that age." Mason couldn't imagine a tiny EvaMarie with no one to hold her, comfort her in her grief.

"It was." Jim met his gaze. "Losing her parents right along with him was even harder."

Mason zeroed his attention in on the other man. "What do you mean?"

"He wasn't always like this, you know. Mr. Hyatt was tough, and had a quick temper, but he loved his kids. Spent loads of time with them...until the day they lost Chris."

Mason instinctively glanced toward EvaMarie but couldn't see her anymore. How confusing must the change in her father have been? On top of never being able to mention the brother she'd idolized...

"It rocked her entire world," Jim murmured, seeming lost in his own memories of that time.

No doubt it had lasting repercussions for her... Mason's own loss at a young age had hit him hard, left lasting scars, and he'd had his brother and father to lean on.

EvaMarie had been all alone.

Suddenly Mason was hit with the realization of

how long they'd been standing there talking…and how quiet EvaMarie was. He glanced over Jim's shoulder again but didn't see her.

Taking his lead, Jim moved away to look behind the open part of the door, then he gestured Mason in with a smile.

Some internal instinct had Mason entering with quiet steps. As EvaMarie came into view, Mason's heart melted. She sat curled against the barn wall in a thick pile of hay, fast asleep. He remembered how she could sleep anywhere, but this had to be a first.

As much as he didn't want to, as much as he wanted to hang on to the distance and anger, Mason couldn't look at her without seeing a gorgeous woman, grime and all. Not only that, he saw a woman who had endured a lot, who had stood on her own two feet without a hell of a lot of support, possibly none.

A woman he wanted the chance to know, even if it was complicated. But he doubted he'd ever be able to see her as the enemy anymore.

Mason glanced toward the stall, listening to the soft sounds of the horses as mama and baby got to know each other. "Everything good here?" he asked.

Jim nodded. "The mare's a pro, and she handled the birth like one." He eyed Mason a moment, then looked over at the sleeping beauty. "I think EvaMarie already has a buyer. The stables will be cleared soon enough. She's gonna miss them though, and vice versa."

Thinking back to what he'd seen when he entered the barn, Mason completely understood. "Once you get the mare settled, text me, then go home."

Jim's eyes widened. "But boss—"

"No." Mason's voice was firm, carrying through the aisle. "You've been here all night. I'm more than capable of watching her." *Both of them.* "Go get some rest. There's nothing here that can't wait until tomorrow. I'll get EvaMarie inside."

"Poor thing is exhausted. When she's devoted, she's all in—and she wasn't leaving until they were both okay."

From what Mason had learned, that sounded about right.

Nine

Carrying a sleeping woman was a unique experience for Mason. He hadn't expected it to be quite so emotional—and it wasn't, not in a soft, mushy way. The feelings rushing through him were fierce, protective and full of demanding need. Add in yesterday's ups and downs and a fitful night's sleep dreaming of this woman's lips, and he had a feeling he was about to be in a very tough spot.

He skirted by the dining room without being noticed by anyone inside. As he climbed the stairs, Eva-Marie began to stir, but didn't open her eyes until they reached the landing.

Even then, a sleepy haze covered her baby blues. They barely opened as he watched her fight her body's normally heavy sleep mode to handle whatever trouble she'd landed herself in now.

If her habit had stayed the same all these years, EvaMarie slept like the dead once she got going.

He carried her to her room, smiling at the feminine touches and soothing green color on the way through to her bath. Once inside, he eased her down onto a little padded bench and kneeled before her, slightly uncomfortable when the comparison to a prince before a princess came to mind.

"EvaMarie, honey, you need to wake up."

Her brow furrowed, but those sleepy blues cracked open once more. "I'm sorry," she murmured, "I'm just so tired."

"Not sleeping will do that to you. But you're also dirty."

Her eyes widened, and she looked down at her dusty clothes. Then he heard a soft sigh. "I almost don't care," she said.

Mason wasn't falling for that. "But you'll blame me when you wake up in dirty sheets, so let's go."

"Go where?" Her lids slid closed, and she slumped toward the wall.

"Oh, no, you don't." Mason pulled her forward with a tiny shake. "EvaMarie, you have to shower."

"With you?"

Mason's world stopped. "What, Evie?"

He saw her eyelids flicker, but it took a minute for her to brave opening them.

"Will you stay with me?" she finally whispered.

His hands tightened, his need to tear through

their boundaries seriously compromising his resolve. "That's not a good idea," he managed to say. "For a lot of reasons."

The barest sheen of tears made her eyes look like damp blue flowers, catching him off guard before she closed them once more. "You're right. I'll be fine."

But *he* wouldn't be.

He hadn't been fine since Evie had come back into his life—and for just a little while, he wanted a taste of what they could be together once more.

Slow but sure, he reached out and started working on the buttons down the front of her flannel shirt.

"What are you doing?"

The simplest answer was the best, because he wasn't entirely sure what he was doing. Going out of his mind, maybe? "Undressing you."

Her breath caught, then she said, "You don't have to do this."

Just as he had yesterday, he reached out and lifted her chin with his knuckles until there was nowhere else for her to look but at him. "No, I don't have to. I want to."

I want you.

Layer by layer he peeled away her clothes; she'd bundled up to keep herself warm. Pulling that last T-shirt over her head to reveal skin and lingerie had him sucking in his breath. Blood and heat pooled low. EvaMarie had filled out into some serious feminine curves. The combination of creamy skin, pink lace and the scent that was uniquely hers sent his heartbeat into overdrive.

This was really happening.

And it looked like he'd found the perfect thing to wake EvaMarie. Though her lashes were lowered, she still watched him. The throb of her pulse at the base of her neck served as a barometer for her response. As did the quiver of her bottom lip.

He eased her to her feet, eager for more. One thing about Mason, once he committed to a cause, he was all in. This time, his entire body agreed.

Before he could get carried away, he turned on the shower to let the hot water work its way up to the second floor. Then he stripped off his own sweatshirt and thermal undershirt. Her eyes drank in every inch of flesh, giving Mason an unaccustomed feeling of pride. He worked hard. His body showed it.

And he was more than happy for EvaMarie to enjoy the results.

Stepping closer, he reached for one of her hands, lifted it for a light kiss, then rested it right over his heart. Suddenly she curled her fingers, scraping her blunt nails against his skin. Just as he'd ached for in the stables.

His body flooded with desire, hardening with need. Soon. Soon.

Without preamble, he unzipped EvaMarie's jeans and shoved every layer beneath down to her upper thighs. He didn't give her time to object, but guided her back down onto the bench and made short work baring her legs and feet. She had shapely muscles—

obviously he wasn't the only one who worked out. And painted toenails—just like always. He grinned at the burgundy polish with gold flecks. A sexy mature choice compared to the neon pinks she'd been into when she was young.

As he lifted her to her feet again, he kissed each of her flushed cheeks. "There's no need to be embarrassed, Evie," he murmured against the smooth slope of her jaw. "This is just you and me."

She curved her fingers over the front of his waistband as if holding on for dear life. "It's been a long time, Mason…you might not like—"

He cut her off with a kiss, tasting her with lips, tongue and purpose. Just as he had last night. Only this time he let the rest of his body join in the game. He tilted slightly, rubbing his chest against lace and skin. The friction drove him crazy. So did the clutch of her hands around his biceps, urging him closer.

He made quick work of his own jeans, but he couldn't bring naked skin to naked skin soon enough. Evie's gasps and groans filled the air. Reaching around her, he placed a hot and heavy palm on each of her butt cheeks to pull her flush against him. The breath seemed to stop in her chest. She held herself perfectly still. His body throbbed hard, demanding more.

"I'm scared, Mason," she murmured.

He knew she spoke the truth, and was probably asking for reassurance at the same time. But this was something she needed to choose willingly.

Stepping back, he retreated out of her reach. Her

expression shattered, but he refused to be swayed. Sliding back the glass door, he stepped into the shower, fighting a shiver when the hot water hit his back, adding to the overload of sensations.

"Join me, Evie," he said, and held out his hand.

Her choice. His chance. His only thought as she took his hand was *hell, yes*.

The last vestige of sleepiness fled as EvaMarie stepped beneath the onslaught of hot water. She'd thought taking off her bra had been hard. But in the steamy space her skin went tight, her nipples even tighter.

How could she want him this much and be so afraid at the same time?

Her desire was dampened by her fear, her self-conscious awareness of the changes in her body and her life. She wasn't a teenager anymore, but she barely had more experience than all those years ago. Would she disappoint him? Would he find her boring?

Still she couldn't walk away from this chance to have Mason one more time. Tears flooded her eyes, forcing her to blink. She needed this. Needed him. He waited patiently, quietly. Though tentative, she reached out her hand to his chest, her eyes closing as she savored the textures of skin and water together.

This was new, exciting. Her heart pounded in her chest; her blood pounded lower. No matter what happened later, she simply couldn't stop.

A step closer, and she couldn't resist glancing up. Mason watched her with a hooded gaze. His body told her he was more than interested. And that look—it conveyed the primal need of an adult male. She was more than happy for him to take what he wanted… so why didn't he?

She caught her bottom lip between her teeth. "Mason?"

"Come to me, sweetheart. Show me what you want."

But that wasn't what she wanted. She needed him to direct, to take…to overpower her so she could stop thinking for once and just feel.

Again he tilted her chin up with his knuckles. She should hate that, resent being manhandled. Instead the gesture made her feel cherished, seen.

"We're gonna do this together, okay, Evie?"

Mesmerized by the intensity in his blue eyes, she nodded.

"Then touch me however you want. Learn whatever you like."

Somehow, his permission loosened her inhibitions. She pressed close, gasping as every inch of her met every inch of him. Slick, steamy, sexy. She explored his body with her own until the friction had her parting her thighs.

Mason took full advantage to thrust his leg between hers. She rose against him, entranced by the feel of hard masculine muscle against her most sensitive skin. Again and again she lifted against him, dragging out the sensations, aided by the guidance of Mason's hands pulling and pushing her hips. His touch added just enough force, and a ton of excitement.

Her whimpers echoed around them. Her body flushed hot as she rode him. With each glide, the friction of his body against her core made her insides tighten with delicious anticipation. Little mini-explosions prepared her for the fireworks to come. Somehow her nails were digging into Mason's shoulders. She should stop, but she couldn't. He wouldn't let her.

Then his hot, open mouth covered the side of her neck, sucking, drawing her orgasm to the surface until she exploded with a cry she couldn't hold inside. His hands pinned her hard against his thigh. His masculine growl vibrated against her sensitive skin, prolonging the ecstasy.

And Mason wasn't about to let that be the end.

He switched places so that her back slammed flush against the tile wall. He rubbed against her, his movements rough, urgent. "Oh, Evie, yes."

Every nerve ending seemed to answer his call. She arched against him, needing, demanding. Lost in sensation, she somehow managed to open her eyes to find his damp drenched blue eyes cataloging her every expression.

"Mason, please," she begged.

His trademark grin made an appearance. "With pleasure." He ripped open the condom packet he'd pulled from his jeans earlier and made quick work of covering himself. His groan as he pulled away for mere seconds made her body soften that much more. He didn't ask, didn't wait for her to comply.

He simply did what he wanted with her. All of her.

Lifting one of her legs at the knee, he hooked his

arm beneath it. Opened her wide. Left her vulnerable to whatever he needed of her. The wall and her hands on his shoulders gave her leverage, but Mason wasn't about to let her fall.

Bending his knees, he made a place for himself right where she wanted him. He eased himself barely inside her. She gasped, tilting her hips in an attempt to accommodate his size. It had been too long. She was embarrassed at how long.

"Easy, baby," he murmured. "Let me make it good."

Just like that, she relaxed. Mason worked his hips, opening her little by little, filling her. The sounds he made lit sparks inside her. His groans, grunts and masculine cries carried the wordless emotions straight to her heart. She pushed her hips toward him, her body now more than eager for his full possession.

As he slid in to the hilt, he moaned through gritted teeth. With a shudder, his whole body strained, his head falling back in a kind of ecstasy that mesmerized her. The pressure between her thighs anchored her to him, to this experience. She thought he would make quick work of it now, driving himself to oblivion.

Instead he paused. Those big hands left her hips to cup her face, and she felt her soul crack a little as his mouth covered hers in a soft, sensual taste that belied the strain of his lower body. His eyes remained open, creating a connection that EvaMarie vaguely thought she might regret later but couldn't turn away from in this moment.

Then he trailed his hands back down, tweaking every sensitive spot along the journey. When he regained his hold, she braced herself for the ride. Sure enough, his body took over, demanding its due.

Every thrust forced her up on her toes, but she didn't notice as sparks flew through her body. She strained with him. Eager. Tense. They both moved on instinct alone until Mason pinned her hip to hip. As their cries mingled in the steam, EvaMarie knew she'd never be the same.

Ten

Horse—check. Workers—check. Food—check.

Mason balanced the tray with care as he made his way back upstairs. The house was not only quiet, it was empty. He'd sent everyone home a couple of hours early tonight, eager to have the place to himself.

What awaited him in EvaMarie's bedroom would be a challenge. He had no doubt.

She'd been asleep before he could get her head on the pillow. So Mason left her to rest while he took care of the work crew and checked a couple of times to make sure Lucy and her foal were getting along well. He knew EvaMarie would want an update when she woke. And hopefully she'd want other things, as well.

But he had a feeling his little filly would be having second thoughts the minute her eyes opened.

He let himself into the darkened room and stood for a moment, soaking in the stillness and the sound of Evie's breathing as she slept. He should be having second thoughts, too. Way more than EvaMarie. So why wasn't he shaking in his boots? Instead he was bringing replenishment to the woman so he could—hopefully—have his way with her again.

God, being with EvaMarie had been nothing like when they were teenagers. Before she'd been tentative, untried. Her hesitation this morning had made him think she'd be the same, but soon she'd been as hot as the water and as responsive as hell. He could still hear her cries echoing off the tiles in the bathroom.

He wanted to hear them again.

Setting the tray on the chaise in her room, he shucked his jeans before easing back the comforter. Suddenly EvaMarie sat straight up. "What are you doing?" she gasped.

Distracted by more bare skin than he'd hoped to see this soon, Mason spent a moment trying to pry his tongue from the roof of his mouth. Noticing the direction of his gaze, Evie gasped again, this time jerking the comforter up over her nakedness. Which was a shame.

He tried to tease her with a grin. "I'm coming back to bed," he said, his voice gravelly with the desire evoked by just the thought of being with her again. "But we can go to my bed if you'd prefer. It's a little bigger. More space for rolling around."

Her eyes widened, and he could just see the images she was tossing around in her mind before she blinked. With innocence overlaying a deep river of sensuality, she was so damn intriguing.

But then panic engulfed her expression. She scrambled back to sit against the padded headboard. "Mason, look, I'm so sorry."

Hmm... Was she sorry she'd slept with him? Because he'd never push her for more than she was willing to give. Or was it something else? This time, her expression wasn't telling the whole story. He let a raised brow speak on his end.

EvaMarie swallowed hard. "I realize you're my employer, and I did not mean to throw myself at you."

Ah, this he could answer. "You didn't."

"I remember asking—" The blush that bloomed over her cheeks was bright enough for him to see in the dim light coming from behind the pulled curtains. Luckily she looked away and didn't notice his smile. He didn't want her to think he was making fun of her. He was simply, well, to his surprise, he was simply enjoying the ins and outs of being with her again.

"And I remember accepting," he finished for her. "I consented way before any clothes came off." He crawled onto the bed to get closer, though he left her with the protection of the comforter. "And I'm really glad I did."

A quick cut of her gaze his way showed him her surprise. "Um. Thank you?"

He chuckled, easing the tension enough for her to meet him face-to-face again.

"Is this gonna be awkward?" she asked.

"Depends."

When she tilted her head to the side, a waterfall of tangled hair spread over her bare shoulder. As the image of burying his face in that silky mass came over Mason, he almost groaned.

But she wasn't done asking questions. "Depends on what?"

"On where this goes now." He flicked his tongue over his suddenly dry lips. "I know what I want, but I'm not gonna push you into anything you don't want to do. Anything that makes you uncomfortable."

"What do you want?" she whispered.

Which only made him think of what other words he wanted her to whisper to him.

"I want the chance to take you to bed."

It wasn't romantic, he knew that. But it was honest. Besides, "romance" and "relationships" came with a lot of complications—especially with EvaMarie.

To his surprise, she said, "On one condition."

This was new. "What's that?"

"That there're no obligations in the end. And no rules as we go."

To Mason's surprise, a trickle of disappointment wiggled through his gut. Why in the world would he be disappointed? EvaMarie was offering him every man's dream—unattached sex with a sensual, beautiful, responsive woman living right in the same house with him. "That's not anything like dating, you know."

She shrugged. "That's not what I'm looking for."

Me, neither. He crawled toward her on all fours, enjoying the widening of her eyes as he stalked her. "But that's two rules, not one."

Her giggle was spontaneous and went straight to his nether regions. He buried his face against her neck. "Then I guess we can have dessert before dinner, right?"

EvaMarie plopped down on the staircase a couple steps up from the bottom. Long minutes of pacing had worn her out, yet parts of her still felt all jittery. The nerves were getting to her.

Mason had left this afternoon to meet with Kane and their lawyer, who had then taken them to dinner. Which was perfectly fine. A weekend in bed together couldn't last forever—nor should she want it to.

She was simply eager for him to see the storage system that had been added to the wine cellar today. That's all.

Oh, who was she kidding? Sure, Mason had been happy to take her up on what she'd offered, and the memory of her request had her face flaming hot. He'd even been complimentary, patient and enthusiastic, which had led to the most incredible two days of her life and done wonders for her ego.

But the minute he'd walked out the door this afternoon, doubt had set in. Her impulsive actions had been the result of a whopper of a few days—the argument with her father, then Mason, then lack of sleep and seeing the foal being born. She certainly hadn't been thinking straight, but couldn't bring herself to regret it.

She simply wasn't ready for it to end.

Since there were no rules, she wasn't sure what to expect. Then tonight, he hadn't come home…no phone call or even a text to let her know where he was after ample time for dinner. Her fingers were crossed Mason wasn't simply avoiding her because he'd had his fill and now he was done.

She shifted on the hard stair. Wouldn't that be a humiliating conversation?

Yes, asking him for some no-strings-attached time had been unprecedented, as well as unpremeditated. But she'd realized that she wanted Mason, without the complications that had come before—and now she could have him.

But for how long?

Mason had agreed…but did he regret his decision the minute he'd left her? Had he told Kane? Were they even now trying to figure out a way to fire her… to get her to leave without angering her enough to file a sexual harassment suit?

Just as her panic reached fever pitch, she heard a key in the front lock. Her stomach clenched hard enough to force her to swallow, but she couldn't tell if it was fear or anticipation. Then she heard—wait, was that a woman?

The wave of nausea rushing over her kept her immobile, so when the door opened she stood and continued to stand there like a scared rabbit, shaking in her sweatpants. *Busted.*

The wave of relief to find herself facing a group of people, and not just Mason with some woman he'd brought home, was short-lived. Because she knew these people. Mason. Kane. John Roberts. And Liza Young.

Liza's gaze swept up the stairs and right to Eva-Marie with her bare feet, baggy sweats and T-shirt. A wave of heat followed that look, lighting EvaMarie with embarrassment everywhere it touched.

"Wow, EvaMarie," the other woman said in an exaggerated drawl. "Whatever are you doing here?"

The heat and nausea combined caused EvaMarie to break out in a sweat. She glanced at Mason, hoping for a little help, but he remained silent, his expression a touch perplexed. Her smile felt sickly, but she offered it to the rest of the group anyway. "Could you all excuse us a moment?"

Surely Mason got her point, but he only went as far as the stairs, even when she moved as if to go farther down the hallway. His frown didn't bode well. Kane and John spoke in a low murmur, but Liza never looked away. With the uncomfortable feeling that her oversized T didn't cover nearly enough, Eva-Marie pulled at the hem.

She returned her attention to Mason, and her nerves flared. "Couldn't you have let me know you were bringing people home?" she snapped.

His right brow shot up. He'd gotten pretty good at the haughty look for someone who hadn't grown up using it. "I didn't realize I needed permission to bring people to *my* house."

Nerves gave way to pain as the remark hit her like a slap to the face. Then a giggle came from right behind Mason's shoulder. They both turned to find Liza listening, her overly mascaraed eyes wide, taking it all in. Her grin turned EvaMarie's stomach, because she'd seen it before—whenever Liza knew she'd just landed a juicy bit of gossip that she could use to her advantage.

"Well, Mason, I thought this was your place now," she said, blinking as if her remark was innocence itself. "But that does make me curious as to what she's doing here..."

Mason glanced back at EvaMarie with a look that said since this situation was all her fault, she could get her own self out of it. Quelling the unexpected urge to smack him, she quietly filled the silence. "I work here."

Liza's exaggerated gasp made EvaMarie want to cringe, but she maintained her stoic expression with the last ounce of her strength.

"Whoa," Liza said, throwing a look around the room as if to include everyone there. "Did y'all hear that? From princess to pauper. Bet that's a big change."

Mason's frown deepened. Luckily this time it wasn't directed at EvaMarie. He turned to face Liza. "Nonsense. EvaMarie knows this place better than anyone," he said. "And she's quite talented with organization and interior decorating."

Kane chimed in too. "She's doing a great job over-seeing the renovations. Let's go look. After all, that's why you're here."

Mason led the way. John Roberts was quick to cross the foyer and offer his arm to Liza, but she was just as quick to get in her parting shot. "Well, she's dressing the part, isn't she?" The words were whispered to her partner, but echoed off the walls of the cylindrical room.

The hitch in Kane's stride said he'd heard, but still he paused right below EvaMarie. "Join us?" he asked.

Words wouldn't come right now. As much as Eva-Marie knew she'd be the object of ridicule every time she met someone of Liza's caliber in the future, that didn't mean it didn't hurt. She was too soft-hearted, her daddy had always said. But truly, it was Mason's response that had hurt her more. If she went with them, she'd probably do something stupid like cry. So she simply shook her head.

The pity in Kane's look quickened her getaway. Her hope to witness the excitement on Mason's face when he saw the new wine cellar pieces didn't matter anymore. Climbing the stairs proved tortuous, as did the whirl of her thoughts. She could go to bed, but Mason would just find her there later—probably crying. Or maybe not.

After all, he didn't seem very interested in her at the moment.

There was only one thing she could think of to soothe herself. A deep breath helped her pull on her big girl panties...along with jeans and a pair of boots.

She'd known she was naïve, but not how much until this very moment.

Now she knew. When Mason said this wouldn't be like dating, he hadn't been lying. This definitely wasn't dating...it wasn't even friendship.

Eleven

Mason gritted his teeth against Liza's inane chatter as he walked their little party back down the promenade to the foyer.

"What, no EvaMarie to see us out like a good girl?" she asked, her giggle scraping Mason's nerves. The glasses of wine she'd had at dinner had combined with the sampling they'd had downstairs to celebrate their renovations, pushing her into the just-inebriated-enough-to-lose-any-claim-to-class stage of drunkenness.

She'd been an unfortunate discovery as John Roberts's dinner companion when their lawyer had introduced them to the stable owner who was also a fellow lawyer. About ten minutes ago, Mason had reached his utmost capacity for stupid and catty remarks for the evening—even if they had learned quite a lot about a few key players in the local upper echelons tonight.

From his increasingly stoic expression, it looked as though Kane felt the same.

"I can't wait to tell the girls that juicy story," the woman rattled on.

"Liza." John Roberts's soft rebuke didn't have any backbone to it.

Mason didn't have the patience to be that soft. His voice came out a low growl. "Excuse me?"

"You know, the whole privileged-daughter-is-now-the-hired-help story," Liza gushed.

Mason had to wonder how long she'd been holding this in. Maybe she'd taken his silence earlier this evening as permission.

"She's always been such a Goody Two-shoes." Liza threw a sly glance at Mason. "At first, I thought maybe she had a totally different reason for being here, but she certainly wasn't dressing to entice anyone, was she?"

Like you would have? Clenching his jaw to keep the words inside, Mason had a sudden epiphany. EvaMarie hadn't been dressed to entice, but she'd definitely been waiting for someone. Crap. That's why she'd been upset that he'd brought people home. She didn't want advanced warning because she felt any kind of ownership over the house or him. She'd wanted the common courtesy of being able to prepare herself before someone came in—something

Mason wasn't used to dealing with, so it hadn't occurred to him.

Man, he'd better get these two out of here before he said something he shouldn't…and gave away more than EvaMarie would appreciate.

Aiming for a distraction, Mason ushered them out the door, then watched as John Roberts gallantly helped Liza down the stairs and out to his car. Halfway across the driveway she ditched her heels, leaving her date to pick up the pieces.

"That woman's laugh could be used as a torture device," Kane said from beside him.

Mason allowed himself a chuckle before turning away from the departing couple. He faced Kane, the man he'd always been honest with. "I screwed up, didn't I?"

"I believe so."

He'd just seen EvaMarie's haughty expression, heard her irritated tone and snapped back in kind. And reacted like the moody teenager he used to be.

Mason stared out into the night as he thought about the implications of tonight's encounter. "Do you think she's told anyone that she's here, working for us?"

"I doubt it." Kane rocked back on the heels of his cowboy boots. "Her parents have taught her the exaggerated importance of preserving her privacy."

"Yeah."

"Did you see her face when Liza made that snide remark about her clothes?"

"No." He hadn't even heard the remark. He'd

been too intent on showing off, which meant getting the others downstairs and away from a situation he wasn't sure how to handle.

"Don't think I've ever seen a face go that blank."

EvaMarie's parents had drilled their version of acceptable behavior into her so thoroughly that making a scene or standing up for herself never would have occurred to her. She'd taken what Liza dished out without a complaint, though he noticed she hadn't joined them downstairs.

"I'd better go check on her," Mason said.

The brothers parted with a quick hand slap, and Kane headed for his truck. Mason went to EvaMarie's room, but she wasn't there. Stumped, he stood on the threshold for a moment.

Maybe she was in Chris's room? After all, he'd bet she was more than upset. But no. She wasn't there either.

You're a smart boy, Mason. Figure it out.

A sudden memory rose of watching a young EvaMarie saddle her horse with tears flowing down her rounded cheeks after yet another dressing down from her father. Did she still love to ride to clear her head? Did she still sit by her favorite tree on the side of the stream that flowed through the middle of the estate into the lake?

He bet she did.

After a quick change into jeans and boots, Mason confirmed his suspicions when he found one of the mares' stalls empty. He quickly saddled up Ruby, groaning as he swung into the saddle. It had been too many days since he'd been on a horse. His growing business activities here cut into his riding time.

He needed to change that.

The ride felt good, free. He moved with the horse, limbering up and clearing his head as he gained speed, though he didn't push the mare too hard in the dark. Since he hadn't been back in the wooded area along the creek as an adult, Mason dismounted and led the horse down the still-clear path he remembered from all those years ago.

The soft whinny of EvaMarie's horse corrected his course just a little. She didn't glance his way as he broke from the tree line. He tied Ruby near Lucy and cautiously approached the blanket EvaMarie was reclining on. "Hey," he said softly, not wanting to startle her if she'd slept through his arrival.

"Hey," she replied.

Which gave him nothing to go on. After all, Eva-Marie had evolved into a master at hiding her emotions. Unsure what else to say, Mason lay down next to her in the darkness. The blanket provided a thick barrier over the mixture of bare dirt and clumps of grass beneath them. The trickle of water from the stream reminded him of the soothing sound when they'd lain here and held each other so long ago. The sky showcased an array of bright stars framed by tree limbs that he didn't remember from his last visit here.

Of course, they hadn't come here for the stargazing back then.

"I wasn't demanding anything from you, Mason," she finally said, her voice sounding huskier, deeper than before. "I don't think I should have to demand the common courtesy afforded to anyone living in the same house—like normal roommates."

Whoa. Though she'd spoken quietly, Mason recognized an unfamiliar tone in EvaMarie's voice. It wasn't even the same tone she'd used when she'd spoken to him in anger the other day. Instead, it was the simple assurance that the facts were in her favor— the facts that called him an overreacting idiot.

Before he could formulate his thoughts, she went on. "I realize that might not be a courtesy given to paid employees—"

"Shush, will ya?"

Leaning up on his elbow, Mason stared at the oval shape of her face, but had trouble making out the details in the dark. "There's no need to play the martyr, EvaMarie."

He rushed on when she opened her mouth to parry with him. "It was thoughtless of me to bring people home without letting you know. Hell, it was thoughtless not to tell you we'd gone to dinner after our meeting, then had drinks. I'm sorry."

She must have been as surprised as he was, because she didn't speak.

"I'm not used to having to think about those things, about other people. Kane and I never had company much except our weekly poker game with the guys. And half of them were stable hands. They just walked in off the job for dinner."

"Thus the poker room, huh?"

* * *

And boy did he.

Drawing her up to her knees, Mason moved in close before she could catch her breath, leaving just enough room for his hands. Very busy hands. All too soon he'd taken her shirt off, and the cool night air kissed her bare skin. The brush of his shirt against the tips of her breasts had her gasping for air.

Then he efficiently removed that final barrier, and heated skin pressed to heated skin. If EvaMarie remembered nothing else from their time together, she knew that first moment of full body touch would stand out above all else.

But she wasn't content to wait on him this time. Her own urgency pushed her to grasp his muscled shoulders, to pull him as close as possible. One of his knees slid between hers, the length of his thigh pressing her jeans roughly against her feminine core. Her moans mingled with the sound of the water nearby and the rush of the wind, all intertwining to heighten EvaMarie's acute senses.

Reaching around, Mason cupped her jeans-clad bottom with his large hands, pulling her up along his leg, then pushing her down until her knees once more touched the ground. The force of his touch and the strain of his body told her this was happening quickly.

His breath deepened, the sound accelerating with the beat of her heart in her ears. His urgency fed her own. Her grip tightened. Her core ached. And her brain short-circuited in her pursuit of making any sense of what was happening.

Better to just feel. Thinking was overrated.

His mouth devoured hers. Nibbling, sucking, exploring. EvaMarie was ready to do a little exploring of her own. Her hands traveled down his back, laying claim to the smooth territory below his waistband. More than enough to overflow her palms, his butt cheeks were squeezable and oh, so sexy. The muscles flexed as he did what he wanted with her body, previewing the dance they would indulge in all too soon.

Suddenly he sucked at her neck, causing everything inside her to tighten—including her fingers. Her nails dug against his skin. In return, he set his teeth against the tendons running along her throat. Their groans filled the air.

"Again," he gasped.

The combined tension and need left EvaMarie light-headed on a runaway train. And she wouldn't have had it any other way.

The same need had Mason fumbling with the button of her jeans. His combined chuckle and growl of frustration floated over her nerve endings like an electrical current. The sheer sensations of being with him like this pulsed beneath her skin.

Within minutes of getting naked, Mason lay back on the blanket. "Take what you want, Evie," he gasped.

To her surprise, the idea inspired her, though her natural hesitation still reared its ugly head.

"Now, Evie."

The force of his words unlocked her barriers. Instead of the slow and careful advance she would have expected, her body leaped into movement. Crawling over him, relief spread through her as she straddled his thighs. Relief, and a rush of desire so strong it was almost a cramp.

Mason was ready for her, but he didn't reach out to help. He positioned himself like a platter on display, eager for her to avail herself of his bounty. So she did. With a single swift move, she made them one. Her entire body gasped at the intrusion, her mind overtaken with the sensation of fullness. Her muscles clasped down in ecstasy.

Mason's moan played over her ears, heightening her experience.

In fact, every response to her movements held her breathless. Never had she felt such a sense of power or responsibility—she could do whatever she wanted with his permission, yet what she wanted was to make it good for him too.

Her body adopted a natural rhythm, one learned through a lifetime of riding. Mason grasped her hands in his, leveraging her up yet keeping them connected. She could watch his face as she moved, learning what entranced him, what ramped up his need and what sent him over the moon.

Before long they were both gasping, playing along the edges of ecstasy without falling over. All too soon, EvaMarie couldn't hold back. She thrust hard.

Once. Twice. The explosion catapulted her into a feeling of flight.

Mason reared up, wrapping his arms tightly around her. His guttural cries against her skin sparked shock waves in the aftermath. A sound EvaMarie knew she'd never forget.

An experience she'd carry with her for a lifetime.

Twelve

"Jeremy, do you know where EvaMarie went?" Mason asked as he stepped into his bedroom.

The crew had repainted the room the day before and was now addressing the crown molding, among other upgrades to the dressing area and adjoining bath.

Jeremy glanced up from his clipboard and blinked, but didn't answer.

"I saw her car leave as I headed back from the barn," Mason prompted.

"Ah, EvaMarie, yes," Jeremy said. "She headed over to the library, I believe."

The library? She'd always been a reader, but— suddenly her father's voice came back to him, *"She got a job at the library."*

Mason tried to continue the conversation casually, but in the back of his mind, unease grew. More than that, his worry unsettled him.

Within twenty minutes he hit the road. The main branch of the town's library wasn't too far from the house. When he entered the building, two librarians eyed him as he walked past, but he continued on his hunt. Finally, a husky, resonating voice led him to... the children's room?

The door to the glassed-in room remained open, but Mason didn't need to stand right on the threshold. EvaMarie's voice carried, so he stood to the right so he could watch her from outside her line of sight. Mason let go of the words and simply focused on the cadence of her voice. As much as he adored that sound, what struck him the most was her expression. Calm. Happy.

She's enjoying herself.

Since his return, the closest he'd seen EvaMarie to happy had been during their discussions about the house, and with the horses. Their most intimate moments together were about a different kind of enjoyment. And he'd seen all too many instances of the blank mask she used to hide her emotions. But this, he could only describe as carefree.

Her guarded look returned as soon as story time ended. Their gazes met through the glass, and Mason could almost see the barriers go up, which told him more than she probably wanted. It meant this place, this time, meant something special to her. Remembering how much she'd loved books when he'd known her before, seeing all the books around her rooms since his return, and her joy in being among these children, he'd have to be completely clueless not to have figured it out.

And he was glad she'd taken steps to create something meaningful in her life.

But her cautious approach said she might not have been ready to share it with him. "Hey. What are you doing here?"

The tone wasn't exactly accusatory. He couldn't put his finger on it, but definitely the caution was there. And for once he wasn't quite sure how to answer... because saying he'd rushed down here because he was afraid she was interviewing for another position would make him more vulnerable than he was ready for.

"Miss Marie?"

Mason looked down to find a little blonde sprite between them. Her arm wrapped around EvaMarie's thigh, as if to claim her in the face of the big bad man across from them. He glanced up at EvaMarie with a questioning look.

"My full name is too much for some of the younger ones to pronounce," she said with a rueful grin.

"Is he your daddy?" the little girl persisted.

"What?" Mason's tone conveyed a wealth of *hell no*.

He immediately recognized his response as a bit too much when a slight wash of tears filled the wide eyes watching him. Unlike him, EvaMarie knew exactly how to handle the situation. With natural ease, she bent down. "He's my friend," she said in a sooth-ing tone. "Like Joshua is your friend."

"Do you play together?"

This one Mason had an answer for... "All the time."

EvaMarie shot him a glare, even as her face flamed.

But the little miss wasn't done yet. "Sometimes Josh will pull my hair."

Mason choked back his laugh as best he could. EvaMarie's skin almost glowed in her embarrass-ment. But this time Mason bent to the little girl's level. "Well, you tell him that's not how girls like to be treated. He needs to be a gentleman and treat you like a lady."

The little girl preened, her smile saying she liked that idea. Then her mother called from across the room, so she hugged EvaMarie quickly and left them with a cute little smile.

"Whew," Mason said, "that was getting tricky."

EvaMarie raised her brow in a nice impression of a Southern belle. "You brought it on yourself."

He had to concede with a grin. After all, he was fully aware of his shortcomings. Instead, he waved a hand toward the rapidly emptying room. "Why this?" he asked.

"My degree is in early education, and this is a helpful way to put it to use," she said as she started straightening up the room.

"Degree?"

Her grin was self-deprecating, but there was also

disbelief mixed in over his surprise. "Yes—believe it or not, I did go to college."

"Oh, I believe it. You always liked to learn." Which reminded him of his one unauthorized visit inside the Hyatt house as a teen. "Is the library still in the turret tower?"

He caught a glimpse of sadness crossing her face right before she turned away to fit the book she'd read back on the shelf. "The room is there, but the movers helped me pack away the books and store them."

She didn't have to tell him she missed it. The turret library had been her favorite room when he'd known her. Her escape, other than the horses.

She turned back to face him, more questions in her eyes, but then her expression changed. "Hello, Laurence," she said, looking over Mason's left shoulder.

"EvaMarie," the other man said, offering Mason a short nod but keeping his gaze on EvaMarie. "I was just down here discussing the Derby festivities for the children's festival." His eyes narrowed. "Could I speak with you, please?"

Mason wasn't sure what came over him exactly. Masculine pride? The burn of competition? But he couldn't stop himself from saying, "Actually we're on our way to lunch. You can call her later." He didn't even look at EvaMarie to see what she thought.

Of course, Laurence wouldn't be a worthy opponent if he didn't protest. "I prefer—"

"Is it urgent?" Mason asked.

"Well, no."

"Then call later." *Or not at all.* Mason hooked his arm through EvaMarie's. "See ya."

Then he ushered her outside.

They were almost to her car when she asked, "Was that really necessary?" Instead of the angry tone he expected after his interference, she sounded almost giggly. He glanced over to see her suppressing a smile.

"Got a problem?" he asked playfully. "Because I can take you back in."

"Right, like I'm looking forward to the lecture I was in for for associating with the... No way." She shot him a look that arrowed straight to his groin— sassy, sexy and something he'd never expected to see from EvaMarie in public. "But I guess this means you owe me lunch."

If this was punishment for opening his big mouth, he'd do it every time. "I'd never dream of going back on my word."

Mason parked on one side of the historic square downtown, and EvaMarie was able to pull into the spot right next to his. They didn't touch as they walked along the sidewalk, but their connection felt almost tangible to EvaMarie. She didn't need his touch to know that he was aware of her, which was an empowering, heady experience.

After last night, she'd felt almost revived, set on a new course, a better course. But she didn't have the overall plan yet.

As they strolled past Mr. Petty's antique shop, something she glimpsed through the window made EvaMarie pause. Her instincts urged her to look closer, check it out, but maybe it wasn't her place to do so. Only she hesitated a moment too long.

Mason joined her. "What is it?" he asked.

So far Mason and Jeremy had been the driving forces behind the renovations. EvaMarie had been present at most of the discussions and had offered her opinion, but never had she taken the initiative. She worried her lip with her teeth for a moment, trying to decide. Finally she offered a small smile. "Let's go inside."

He nodded and held the door for her. Stepping across the threshold to the jingle of the doorbell, EvaMarie made her way straight to the piece she'd seen through the window: an old-fashioned sign for a gentleman's sports lodge, weathered with age, but in good repair. She pointed to the sign. "Mason, wouldn't that be great in the poker room?"

"Hell, yeah." He grinned up at the sign. "This is perfect. Good eye."

She tried to ignore the glow of pleasure blooming in her belly. "We could carry the dark wood theme from the wine cellar into the game room, kind of give it a hunting lodge-type feel."

"I've got more where that came from, if you're interested."

EvaMarie turned to see the proprietor had found them. "We're decorating a game room. What did you have in mind?"

Half an hour later, they had purchased the sign, wall rack, poker table and wine rack in varying degrees of restoration. It was a job well done. It felt good, and Mason's deference to her opinion left Eva-Marie glowing.

They continued down the sidewalk to a popular corner café at a casual stroll. "So where did you go to college?" Mason asked.

"An exclusive women's liberal arts college in Tennessee. Father wanted me to study so I would be articulate and ladylike, but he didn't really care what else I actually learned there, so I decided on something I thought I would enjoy doing one day." How different she'd dreamed her life would be, even then. "By the time things went downhill and I needed to get a job, my degree was years old. I'd need some updating and to pass my teaching certification exam. There was always so much to do, I just never seemed to find the time to enroll."

Many people, Mason included, saw her from the outside and expected days filled with directing staff and having her nails done. When the actuality of running a household, caring for a sick parent, and bolstering up another weak parent were like two full time jobs in only one twenty-four-hour period. "What about you?" she asked, curious about Mason's life after he'd moved away.

"I majored in business management. Dad insisted, even though I didn't see the point in a full four-year degree. We always knew we wanted to run our own stables, and had plenty of hands-on knowledge, so

I thought shorter, more specific studies would be more appropriate."

He smiled at the hostess as she seated them. To EvaMarie's surprise, he took the chair right next to her instead of the one across from her, bringing them closer, creating a more intimate atmosphere that matched their conversation. She forced herself not to acknowledge the tingles low in her core at his nearness, his attention.

Seemingly unaware, Mason went on. "Now I know why he did so many things I didn't understand. Kane and I both needed the knowledge, ways of thinking and maturity that came from college to not only maintain our own businesses, but build the reputation that will help sustain us in such a public arena."

"And then you cut your teeth on the stables back home."

Mason nodded, then smiled at the waitress as she delivered their drinks and an appetizer of fried green tomatoes with corn-bread muffins. He waited until she'd taken their lunch orders to answer. "We started those stables with our dad. There's also some cattle ranching, but it's not a huge herd because the property isn't big enough to sustain it. Our big focus there is horse breeding. As we developed those lines, we were on the lookout for stock that would be our start into racing. I'm proud to say our dad helped us pick out our first mare and stud."

The smile they shared felt like more—more personal, even intimate in the midst of a crowd. What they were discussing might have seemed mundane, but EvaMarie knew how much it meant to Mason. She remembered him talking about running his own stables when he was a teenager, and had watched him soak in everything the other stable hands and manager had been willing to teach him.

As much as it saddened her to leave her home, she could actually see that it would be in good hands with the Harrington boys. "You're gonna do great," she murmured.

Surprise lit up his eyes. "Your dad would call that kind of talk sacrilege."

"Of course he would. That doesn't make it any less true."

His gaze held hers. "Thank you. That means a lot to me."

The very air between them seemed to grow heavy, leaving EvaMarie breathless and a little confused. Mason blinked, then focused on the plate in front of them. He snagged one of the tomatoes and lifted it toward her lips. "Taste this. I had some the other day, and they're great."

She wasn't about to tell him the treat was nothing new to her. Instead, she clamped down on her surge of need as he fed her the crispy tart bite, then took one of his own. Definitely not the kind of response she should be having in public.

"Well, this doesn't look much like business. Now does it?"

Liza's cutting, accusatory tone belied the saccharine smile plastered on her face as she stood beside their table. How long she'd been there, EvaMarie couldn't have said. She'd been too caught up in the magic of Mason's attention.

Silence reigned for a moment. After last night, Mason was probably afraid to touch the remark with a ten-foot pole, so EvaMarie adopted a closed expression and answered just loud enough for the group of women watching from a few feet away to hear her. "We just finished buying the decor for the new game room at the shop next door. Antiques will give the room real depth, I believe. Don't you agree?"

Liza's eyes widened, as if she didn't know how to take this polite response to her tasteless interruption.

"I agree," Mason finally chimed in. "Mr. Petty has some unique pieces in his store. I'll probably go back for other things for the house, but what we ordered today is perfect for that room." The grin he offered Liza sparked some nasty jealousy, but Eva-Marie ignored it. Because Mason wasn't hers to be jealous over.

"Still a man cave," he went on, "but with class."

The attention helped Liza recover. She offered him a smile seemingly loaded with double meaning. "As if you could be anything but classy." Stepping a little closer, she rested her hand on Mason's shoulder. Her red nails seemed to dig just a touch. EvaMarie might have been imagining that from this angle. But she wasn't imagining the husky quality that colored Liza's voice. "I had such a good time last night."

I'm amazed she remembered it...

Meeting Mason's gaze with her own, EvaMarie

could have sworn she saw the same thought reflected there. He gave a slight nod and her heart pounded. Being on the same wavelength with him was certainly a heady experience. Then he turned back to look up at Liza.

"How's John Roberts?" he asked.

Liza frowned. "How should I know? He dropped me off after a lecture on—" Stopping abruptly, she flicked her gaze between Mason and EvaMarie, then shook her head. "Anyway, I haven't seen him today. The girls and I are just out for some shoppin' and strollin'."

"Well, I see the waitress headed this way with our lunch," Mason said, "so if you don't mind…"

Sigh. What woman couldn't see that Mason wasn't interested? Of course, just the thought made EvaMarie worried that she was also the type of woman who read more into what was happening between her and Mason than what was really there. Things she really shouldn't want but couldn't quite turn away from.

"Of course," Liza said, never taking her eyes from him. "But I do hope you'll remember that preseason party we're having. It's gonna be the biggest thing around here. Anyone who is anyone will be there. Please tell me you'll come."

"You said you hadn't even sent out the invites yet."

The other woman's sweet smile made EvaMarie slightly sick.

"Mason, dear, you don't need an official invite. You're welcome anytime."

After her parting salvo, Liza turned without a

goodbye and headed for the table her shopping companions had claimed...right within line of sight. Mason ignored the final part of the conversation and dug into his food with the gusto of a hardworking man.

But EvaMarie was left with the knowledge of the role reversal between them. For the first time, he was invited to the party she wouldn't be considered good enough to attend.

Thirteen

"Girl, aren't you about done with all this work for the day?"

EvaMarie gasped, her heart automatically jumping at the sound of a man's voice despite knowing Mason was out of town. "Don't scare me like that!" she scolded Jeremy.

He leaned against the threshold to what used to be the walk-in closet off her dressing room—now her sound studio. "You know you're too protective of this," he said. "If you'd just tell Mason, he'd fix it so you could continue to work here."

She looked around the surprisingly roomy space. At least, it was roomy for what she needed. When she'd started creating the studio, she'd given away and stored tons of clothes that she'd held on to since she was a little girl. Her current wardrobe resided on a portable rack in her dressing room.

In here, she'd stripped the walls down to the Sheetrock and installed a layer of insulation. She'd planned to refinish the walls, but then Mason had bought the estate. The space left provided enough room for a small desk that held her recording equipment, scripts, a small lamp and office supplies.

Just what she needed to build her career narrating audiobooks.

She'd never brought Mason in here, and he'd never asked.

What she was trying to do here, and the hope it represented for a new life, a new independence, felt fragile to her. Mason had always gone after whatever he wanted and damn the consequences. He'd probably see her efforts as weak, shadows of his own mighty conquests. Hopefully she could finish out her time in her childhood home without having to expose this part of herself.

It was the very first thing that was all her own. Her parents didn't know. Neither Laurence nor any of her friends knew. Jeremy had only divined the truth after wiggling his way in. To her surprise, he'd become her fiercest cheerleader. She simply hadn't been able to share it with Mason yet. It was too personal, too risky. If she failed, she wasn't gonna do it in front of an audience. "I know things aren't going to end well with him," she argued. "They can't. This, I mean, I haven't even told my parents about this. How could I—"

"You gotta have positive thoughts, girlie."

"No." She turned his way, giving him a hard glare. "No positive thoughts. Not in this. My father almost ruined Mason's family. No matter how much of a good time we're having..." She stumbled over the words.

Jeremy gave her a knowing grin. "And a very good time it is, indeed."

"Shush. It won't last." She glanced around the small room. "This—I need in my life. I need to accomplish this, to support myself, okay?"

"So if this thing with Mason isn't gonna last, why do you have this out?"

From the rack beside the door, Jeremy lifted up a formal dress in a garment bag. EvaMarie's heart thudded. Jeremy knew what the dress was—they'd discussed it when the movers were cleaning out a storage room downstairs. She should have sent it to the storage unit, but she hadn't been able to. She shouldn't have tried it on, but she hadn't been able to resist. She shouldn't have had it cleaned this week, but she hadn't been able to quiet the hopeful voice inside that said Mason would ask her to go to Liza's family's ball the day after he returned.

She knew he had a new suit. She'd taken delivery on it when it had arrived.

"I don't even know why I have it out. He hasn't mentioned taking me." She slumped into her chair, disgust rolling through her to wash all the starch from her posture. "Why am I torturing myself like this?"

Because this had been the best few weeks of her

life. No parents to judge or criticize her. Purpose and meaning in her work. And a man who made her feel sexy and wanted.

Even if he didn't really want her for the long term.

"So just go yourself and show him what he's missing," Jeremy said.

Her grin was rueful. "Can't. I didn't get an invitation. Except—"

"Except what?"

"Laurence has asked me to go with him, as a friend."

Jeremy was already shaking his head. "Don't do it."

"I'm not." But she wasn't sure that she wouldn't. The thought of Mason being there without her, not even realizing he could have invited her, stung. She might just be selfish enough to give in to Laurence.

Jeremy lifted the bag once more. "This would fit you perfectly. And there's nothing wrong with hoping, EvaMarie."

"Except feeling shattered when your dreams don't come true," she replied, but her tone held little heat. Deep inside, a small part of her was already resigned to never finding someone who would accept all of her, including her family obligations and who she truly was and wanted to be as a person. Those guys seemed few and far between.

But it was the dream dress—her mother's from her "debut" on the local scene. It fit EvaMarie perfectly... Who was she kidding? She wasn't going to any stupid dance, so she should stop mooning around about it like a teenage girl from an after-school special.

"Did you need me?" she finally asked, doing her best to forget the complications and focus on reality.

"Do you have time to show me where the furniture needs to be placed in the study?"

"Yeah. I've got about an hour's worth of recording left, but I need to give my voice a break first."

Her current project was a blessing in many ways. It had come in the same day Mason had left to go out of town—it was also her longest project to date, by an author she'd never worked with before, so she hadn't been entirely certain how many hours would be involved. But the author was a bestseller with lots of connections. If she liked EvaMarie's work, this could lead to some good things for her budding career.

But she'd delayed jumping into the project because she'd been nervous about doing a good job. A few false starts, though, and she'd been ready to go.

Jeremy glanced over the equipment she'd painstakingly paid for, piece by piece, and treated like the most delicate of babies. "I think this is so cool," he said. "With your voice and attention to detail, you're gonna be a star."

"I'll settle for financially stable, but thank you."

She was gonna miss the little studio when she was forced to move. Despite the half-finished walls and need for secrecy, the alternative would likely be a tiny closet or bathroom in an apartment complex, with all the noise complications that came with it, so—

"You should still tell him," Jeremy said, nagging her. "I thought you were moving into a whole I'm-going-after-what-I-want stage of life?"

The reminder had her standing up straighter, but she knew the minute she looked into Mason's eyes, her words would die unspoken. She enjoyed having sex with him—hell, that was an understatement. And not just the physical part, but the exploration and intimacy of being with Mason. She even enjoyed living with him—his smart, funny approach to life kept her guessing and on her toes.

But she refused to use the L word. Because if she couldn't trust Mason with the most important things in her life, like the career she was struggling to build book by book, then he wasn't truly the man she wanted for forever.

Was he?

EvaMarie took a deep breath and braced herself before she even stepped out of her car. The doors of the assisted living center where her parents now resided weren't quite far enough away for her liking. She hadn't seen her parents since the blowup at the restaurant. Heck, she'd barely even talked to her mom, and not at all with her dad.

Maybe she should put this off for another day?

But her mother had needed a few things from storage and given her a few niggling reminders that EvaMarie hadn't been to see the place since they'd gotten settled and—boom! Here she was...

I'm such a sucker.

Trying for a positive attitude, she pushed through the door with purpose and smiled at the girl behind the reception desk who directed her to the Florida room. According to her mother, their new afternoon routine included cool drinks with friends before dressing for dinner. Her parents were happy. Settling in. Her job was done.

Except walking through the spacious rooms with their lush, real plants and unique pieces of artwork only heightened the sense of pressure to perform. Her parents couldn't truly afford to live here without digging deep into the savings that needed to stay untouched in case of a rapid decline in her father's health. So EvaMarie was supplementing his disability checks.

Something she'd need to continue doing, which meant achieving her goal of becoming a successful voice artist was of the utmost importance. And after her time with Mason was done, she'd probably have to take another part-time job, as well. Some days she thought she would never know what it was like to live without the performance pressure.

"EvaMarie, there you are," her mother said as soon as she reached the door. Her mother met her halfway with a kiss. "Darling," she murmured, "you couldn't have dressed up a bit more?"

Since when was she required to "dress" to visit her parents? She'd thought her jeans and nice shirt were perfectly presentable.

They approached a table where several other residents were seated. As soon as her mother started to introduce everyone, EvaMarie changed her mind. Maybe dressing up would have bolstered her confidence in the face of so many people. Her father rose to stand beside her, an arm around her shoulders. It was a pose they'd adopted many times through the years. The picture of the perfect family.

To EvaMarie, it only reminded her just how far from perfect they were.

"If you all will excuse us a moment," her mother said, "I wanted to introduce EvaMarie to Mrs. Robinson."

EvaMarie moved along with a smile, then said, "Mother, I really need to bring in your clothes and stuff—"

"Nonsense. There's plenty of time for that."

They came to a table closer to the floor-to-ceiling windows occupied by an elderly woman. She appeared awfully frail, but her expression was alight with intelligence when she turned to them. At her direction, they were seated and her father flagged down a waiter for a round of iced sweet tea.

"You were absolutely right, Bev," Mrs. Robinson said. "Your daughter is beautiful."

EvaMarie murmured her thanks, while her mother beamed. Though it made EvaMarie feel like she was three, the compliment pleased her mother. After chatting for a few minutes, her father stood. "Bev, let's go arrange to move your things to our apartment."

But when EvaMarie started to rise, he waved her back. "We can take care of it. You stay and chat."

"Um…" Her parents seemed all too happy to

make a hasty retreat. But the silence wasn't awkward for long.

Mrs. Robinson chuckled. "They aren't subtle, those two, that's for sure."

"I'm so sorry."

"Don't be, child. I did actually want to meet you, and now that I have, I'm very glad." Her smile softened the angular edges age had added to her face. "In this instance, I think your mother was dead right."

"About what?" EvaMarie asked, caution leaking into her voice.

"Why, I'm looking for someone to hire to take care of my place."

Surprised, EvaMarie stared for a moment. "Your place?"

"Yes, child. I had to move here about six months or so ago when I started having some bad back issues. My nephew has been staying at my home since then. Keeping everything in good repair and making sure no one starts thinking it's empty."

"That's nice of him."

Mrs. Robinson laughed again. "Well, I paid him to do it. I don't expect anyone to uproot themselves out of the goodness of their hearts. Plus, the house is a good enough size and filled to the brim with antiques, so there's always something that needs looking after. But now he's been offered a really good job in Nashville, and I need someone to take his place."

EvaMarie stilled. "You want to pay me to watch over your house?"

"Well, you'd need to live there. Your parents mentioned you would need to move out of your own situation posthaste. That's perfect for me. Not that I expect you to give up your normal activities. Just stay on top of things and come out here once a week for us to go over what's happening and any expenditures."

Mrs. Robinson glanced over EvaMarie's shoulder. "Ah, I see your parents heading this way, so I'll hurry. Despite what they may say, dear child, there's no pressure. But if you think you'll be interested, please let me know soon. You can call the front desk and ask them to transfer your call to my suite."

She reached across the table with one frail hand, prompting EvaMarie to take it. "You let me know. All right?"

EvaMarie had to clear her throat to get her words out. "Thank you, ma'am."

"My pleasure," the elderly woman said just as EvaMarie's glowing parents returned.

Another fifteen minutes of casual conversation was punctuated by her parents casting pointed glances her way. Somehow EvaMarie managed to ignore them, and Mrs. Robinson gave her a pleased nod as they left. They didn't even make it around the corner before her mother started in.

"Isn't it a wonderful opportunity?" she gushed. "The old Robinson place is one of those gorgeous antebellum homes in the historic district. Very prestigious looking. You couldn't ask for a better situation."

"I thought you didn't want me taking care of other

Fourteen

Mason frowned as he waited one more time for EvaMarie to answer her phone. He'd called twice already—once at dinnertime, then again a couple of hours later. Both calls had gone straight to voice mail.

If everything hadn't been just fine when he'd left, he'd think she was avoiding him.

"Hello?"

Boy, one breathless word and Mason was wishing away the hundreds of miles between them. How had he become addicted this hard this fast? "Hey," he replied, his own voice deepening with his desire.

She didn't speak, and her very hesitation magnified his uneasiness from earlier. He focused on the sound of her breathing. "How has your day been?" he finally asked.

Oh, that deep sigh could mean so many things.

"Well, Jeremy's crew completed the first-floor tiles."

Mason had known the job was next on the list, but he hadn't expected them to get to it this quickly. "That's great."

"Yes. But I finally had to leave," she said with a soft chuckle. "I couldn't handle the sound of them cutting. No matter where I hid, that high-pitched whine chased me down."

The noise could be piercing. Not to mention the commotion caused by the extra crew Jeremy had brought in to get the entire floor done quickly. Good thing Mason had been out of town. "So did you ride out to the stream so you could fantasize about me?"

His little joke didn't garner him the laugh he was looking for. "Actually, I went to visit my parents."

"Bummer."

"Mason."

How could even her preschool teacher voice sound sexy? "Hey, you know you need someone to brighten your day. I'm just trying to help that along."

Her huffy sigh expressed a depth of exasperation that told him his playful mood was not winning him any points. He probably shouldn't ask if they'd spent the entire time lecturing her on quitting her job. Maybe he'd try a different tactic.

"I actually did want to talk to you about something."

"Really?"

He grinned as excitement entered her voice, softening the irritation.

"Yep. Kane and I have a new job for you."

"Oh."

Mason rushed on, his enthusiasm for their idea pushing to the surface. "We've decided to host a big bash at the house. After all, there will be a lot to show off, right? Introduce ourselves to the racing community, entertain in the new spaces downstairs, have a buffet in the formal dining room…" It took a while for him to realize that EvaMarie wasn't responding. "What do you think?" he demanded.

"If being seen is what you want, that will make a big splash."

"We need to be seen and make contacts…it's good for business."

"This will definitely be good for business."

So why didn't she sound excited? "We want you to put it together for us. I told Kane that no one would know better what to have and who to invite. You'll do great."

"Sure."

Maybe she was simply overwhelmed. "I know you've got a lot going on with the renovations, but this will be fun. And great for us."

"It will be my pleasure to organize a party for you."

But it didn't sound like a pleasure. Her voice was stiff, not husky and molten like when he usually spoke with her. Maybe he should change tactics. "I think I'll be back by Thursday."

She was silent so long he wondered if they'd been disconnected. "EvaMarie, are you okay?"

"Sure." She still didn't sound convincing, but at least she was talking. "I'm just tired, I guess. A lot on my mind."

"Anything I can help with?"

"I doubt it."

He wasn't sure, but he had a good guess what the problem was. After all, in twenty minutes her parents had totally screwed up his head. He could only imagine what they could do to hers in an afternoon. "Did you spend all day fighting off new suitors or better job offers?"

"No," she snapped back. "Nothing like that."

"Come on...work with me here," he crooned. He'd never seen her in this kind of mood, but he was more than up for the challenge. "I'm very good at distraction."

"And that's helping, how?"

"Do I look like Dr. Freud? Don't kill the messenger. I'm not the obsessive worrier here, am I?"

Now he garnered a laugh, small one though it was. "Well, I can't deny it, as much as I'd like to."

"See?" It felt good to make her feel good, even over the phone. Almost as good as making her feel awesome in person.

And she wasn't letting him off the hook. "Well, if you want to help, you may need to work a little harder."

"Oh, I'm perfectly capable of working it hard if

you need me to." He let his voice deepen into a playful growl.

"Mason!"

There we go. Time to have some fun. "Well, maybe not from this far away...but I can make it work for you."

"What did you have in mind?" That breathlessness from earlier had returned. Even though they were only connected by phone, her husky voice worked its way along his nerve endings to set them all abuzz.

"Just talking. You like talking to me, right?"

"Of course."

Her response was too matter-of-fact. He needed to shake her up. "Then tell me your favorite part of what we do together."

"Um, what?"

She sounded so innocently shocked he wanted to laugh...or kiss her thoroughly. "Come on, baby. Tell me what you like." His body throbbed as he waited for her answer.

"I don't know," she whispered, leaving silence to hang between them.

"I'm waiting."

"When you..." He heard her clear her throat. "When you kiss and suck at my neck," she finally murmured.

Mason's mind conjured up explicit details of him doing just that. "And I love how you respond. Moaning. Nails digging in. Your hips lifting to mine."

Every word brought a new picture. His body tightened, and he desperately wished she were there for him to hold close right now.

She felt it too. He could tell by the acceleration in her breath. Was she eager to play? "Now tell me how you like to be touched."

"With hands…" she said, quicker now to respond, "hands that are rough, calluses on them."

Just like his.

"Firm. Guiding me. Supporting me."

Just like he wanted to.

"Digging in." Her voice was almost deep enough to be a moan. "Not to hurt, but in the excitement of the moment."

Just like his did when he felt her climax around him.

Mason broke out in a sweat, hands clenching into tight fists. Not from the images she was conjuring. But from the fear that after playing with fire, he'd never again be free of his need for EvaMarie.

"I thought we agreed you wouldn't go to the ball with Laurence?"

EvaMarie paused in her attempt to work one of her amethyst earrings into the hole in her ear. She hadn't worn them in forever. There wasn't any need for fancy jewelry at the few places she went. But they went perfectly with her mother's debutante dress, so EvaMarie hadn't been able to resist.

"I'm not, actually," she replied to Jeremy. The frown that appeared on her face in the mirror didn't go with the filmy cream layers of her dress or the elegant upsweep of her hair. Why did he have to ruin her anticipation? She was having a hard enough time hanging on to her composure as it was.

She caught the pointed look he directed her way via the hall mirror. "I'm going on my parents' invite, okay? They insisted. I might be meeting Laurence there, just as friends."

After all, how pathetic would she look without a date? And the fact that she had to worry about that, when she had a man who had no problem climbing into her bed every night, ticked her off.

"But you're really going to be spying."

"I don't know," EvaMarie said. Her frustration from the past week boiled over. "He didn't say if he was going, okay? Didn't say if he was coming home tonight. Didn't give me any indication whether me going with him was even an option at all." She huffed, blinking back tears. After all, she didn't want to ruin her mascara.

At least, that's what she told herself.

"Why didn't you ask?" Jeremy said.

Ask? "Why didn't I ask? Because wouldn't that leave me looking pathetic when he said no?"

"So it was easier not to ask than it was not to know?"

"I…" Maybe so. Maybe not. "I'm just confused."

Jeremy moved in close, looking suave and elegant in the mirror in spite of the casual clothes he wore for working on the estate. He settled warm hands on her bare shoulders. "Sweetheart, you are worthy

of an answer. If you don't get one, you have to demand one."

"But—I can't..." In her world, demands were always punished. "That's just not me."

"Isn't it? Isn't that what this is all about?" He
waved a hand over her dress. "A way to demand
Mason answer your unspoken questions without having to come right out and ask them?"

Her hands clenched into the gown at her sides, as
if fearful someone would try to tear it from her. "Are
you saying this is wrong?" she asked.

"Absolutely not," Jeremy said, meeting her gaze
in the mirror. "I just don't want you to sell yourself
short. Have some self-respect, EvaMarie. You've
earned it the hard way. But you'll never build up
your stockpile if you keep letting people steal it from
you..."

The image that statement created in her mind held
her in awe for a moment. She could literally picture
a pile of gold bars that her father and mother and
Mason and Liza all kept stealing from...and she did
nothing to stop them.

"All right," she said, a glimmer of understanding
rapidly expanding in her mind. "I just want to see if
something happens...if he responds. Wouldn't you?"

Her restlessness this week had coalesced into a
fierce curiosity to see just how Mason would react
to her in a public setting. After all, they weren't dat-
_____ _____ _how, some way, she'd still thought he
_____ __ _o to Liza's ball with him.
_____ _ointed.

But she didn't know the why of it—at least, a why that she could accept. That's what was eating at her. Along with the job offer she'd had. She hadn't been able to bring it up with Mason…but she needed to make a decision before the opportunity slipped through her fingers.

Jeremy kissed her on her temple. "Girl, yes, I would." He squeezed her arms to encourage her. "You look beautiful, sweetheart. I just don't understand why you think things couldn't work out with Mason. Any man would be lucky to have you."

EvaMarie shook her head, blinking back tears. "It can't work. There's too much history, too much—"

"Seems to me like it's working now. I don't see what the past has to do with anything."

She met his gaze straight up. "Can you honestly see my father walking me down the aisle to meet Mason? I'm not ready to spend a lifetime separated from the parents I still love."

Like Mason's mother. Had it been wrong of her to walk away from her family for love? Had she regretted it? EvaMarie knew her parents would be the same, forever condemning her for that choice. But then again, they might not cut her off completely. They'd become quite dependent on her these past few years.

If her parents weren't an issue, would she make a different choice?

"I'll see you at the party," Jeremy said, turning to go as if he knew he'd said enough.

She nibbled on her l

echoed down the hallway and then down the flight of steps to the basement.

She could tell herself she was going because she wanted to, but deep down, she knew what she really wanted was to see Mason there—and be seen by him. But she did have some pride. If he ignored her, she would not push the matter.

To make her nerves worse, Mason hadn't made it home the day before as planned. She knew he was heading out sometime today, but he hadn't said when, hadn't called her when he left, nothing. So this was probably just a tournament of nervous tension for nothing.

Stop mooning and go if you're going.

So she did. Only stepping out of her car was a bit more difficult than she'd anticipated. After all, she'd always come to these events *with* her parents or *with* Laurence. Never on her own. And people could talk about lifting your chin and storming a room with pride...but it was actually a damn hard thing to do.

But she pictured that pile of gold bars and knew she didn't ever want to be with someone who wouldn't add to that pile. Which meant, if she were to continue living with herself, she better get to work.

Because she was worthy of way more than a pile of gold. She was worthy of respect—and tonight she would demand it.

Fifteen

Mason stumbled, exhausted, into the side entrance when he got home around seven on Friday. Over twenty-four hours after he should have been here. He hadn't even been sure he'd make it in tonight. The long drive over, after some last-minute meetings this morning, had about done him in. But as much as he wanted to hole up underneath EvaMarie's cozy down comforter, he needed to put in an appearance at Liza's party.

Kane hadn't been able to leave at all, making it all the more imperative that Mason serve as the lone rep for their debut tonight in Kentucky racing circles. Liza's family was both prominent and well-connected in the local racing scene. Mason needed to get his name—and even better, his face—circulating.

But first, he wanted to see EvaMarie. She hadn't sounded right when he talked to her on the phone yesterday, and something told him she was upset. Hopefully not with him, but she hadn't wanted to talk about it. He could tell by the hesitation in her responses and how distracted she'd sounded.

EvaMarie wasn't the type to spill her guts, even after all they'd shared. If Mason wanted to know, he'd have to coax it out—something he hadn't wanted to do over the phone. He was much better at it in person.

He looked around the downstairs, noting the sleek elegance of the new tiled floors and the finished dining room. No sounds came from the basement, so Mason assumed they were done for the day, though Jeremy's car was still in the drive.

Mason took the stairs two at a time, hoping to find EvaMarie in her room, but all was quiet. As he searched, the ticktock of time passing niggled in his brain.

No EvaMarie. Maybe she was in the barn. Would she be able to shower quickly and throw on a dress? Did she even own a formal dress? Surely she did, but he wasn't sure how long it had been since she'd worn one.

He'd spent years dreaming of her living the high life on her parents' money. But in actuality, her life had been very different.

In clear detail, Mason now saw the drawbacks to his decision not to mention the party to EvaMarie. He might have been worried he wouldn't make it home, but if she was here somewhere, he hadn't left her a lot of time to get ready.

Of course, he'd also felt some confusion over whether he should ask her at all. Despite the incredible intimacy they shared, they weren't technically dating. They'd agreed on that. Mason didn't want her to feel like she had to go with him if she wasn't comfortable making a public appearance on his arm.

But by God, he wanted her with him tonight.

He reached into his pocket for his phone to call her, all while stomping across her rug to the dressing room he knew was on the other side of her bathroom. As he entered the room, he saw a rack of clothes to one side, which seemed odd. No formal dresses there, though. He reached for the door to the closet. Maybe she kept things she didn't wear much in here.

But what he found inside had nothing to do with clothes. What the hell?

"Girl, why are you back already? Did you forget something?" Jeremy called from the bedroom. "Or did the thought of facing an evening with dull Laurence make you change your mind?"

Ducking back out of the closet, Mason came face-to-face with the other man.

"Oh, snap," Jeremy said. He swallowed hard. "I don't think you're supposed to be in there."

"It's my house," Mason said, stalking closer. His exhaustion faded in the face of his growing anger. "I can be wherever I want."

Jeremy inclined his head, holding his hands up in surrender. "Also true."

"What's this?" Mason asked, jerking his head back toward the closet.

The walls had been covered in insulation, and the shelves were empty of clothes. A table and a filing cabinet had replaced the closet's usual function. If he had to guess, what looked like sound equipment was the key to the mystery.

Jeremy worried his lip as his averted gaze told Mason he didn't want to answer.

"You obviously know," Mason said. "Spill it. Does princess have a ham radio obsession I'm not aware of?"

Jeremy laughed, then slapped a hand over his mouth. When he finally removed it, he was sober under Mason's glare. "Well, she has an incredible voice, right?"

Mason couldn't argue that. "What does that have to do with—"

"She needs a way to support herself," Jeremy rushed to say. "A mutual friend of ours is an author, and she put EvaMarie in touch with some people in the audiobook industry. She's been working very hard to build a foundation…"

Jeremy's voice trailed off as he noticed Mason staring. Mason couldn't help it. His brain had short-circuited the minute he'd realized EvaMarie was building a career. Not a job, not a hobby. A career. One she hadn't bothered to mention to him—at all.

"Where is she?" he demanded, not caring that his voice had roughened.

He could tell from Jeremy's face he wasn't going to like this answer either.

"She left about forty-five minutes ago for Liza's party."

Liza's party. Without him. Yet another thing she hadn't mentioned. "With dull Laurence?"

Jeremy shook his head but paused under Mason's look. "Well, she drove herself, but she was meeting him there. As friends."

Mason gave a sound of frustration and anger all mingled together.

For once, Jeremy didn't pause. "Well, what did you expect, man? *You* certainly didn't invite her."

No. No, he hadn't. He'd thought to keep everything separated into neat little compartments. But that didn't mean he wanted to hear about it from someone else. "I don't think I need you to tell me how to handle this—" He'd almost said relationship, but that wasn't what he had with EvaMarie, was it? Not really.

"Well, you certainly need someone to tell you," Jeremy said, gaining bravado and not backing down beneath Mason's glare. "She's not just your housekeeper, now, is she? She's your woman...or is she just convenient?"

Shock jolted through Mason. "Is that what she thinks?"

"Should she?"

"Should I?" Mason demanded, gesturing back toward the modified closet.

Jeremy frowned. "I'm sure she has her reasons for

keeping certain things private, but I think EvaMarie isn't the only one who needs to be honest around here."

Mason wanted to rail some more, work out his aggression here and now. As if he knew that, Jeremy didn't even give him the chance. He simply left.

Mason glanced back into the darkened room with its pile of sophisticated equipment. He'd kept business and pleasure and emotions completely apart from one another. Like a picky child who thought the piles of food on his plate would contaminate each other if they touched. Obviously Mason had been too good at keeping things separate. And while he could forgive EvaMarie for going to the party without him, he refused to take responsibility for her keeping this a secret. That was all on her.

And Mason wanted an explanation.

EvaMarie slowly relaxed into the rhythm of the evening. Laurence had been just attentive enough when she had arrived to soothe her secret ego, but seemed to lose interest quickly. Which wasn't unusual for him. Her parents had been welcoming, without finding any little faults to disapprove of... All in all, she was having a much better time than she'd expected.

Except for the urge to look toward the entryway every ten minutes to see if Mason was going to show up.

She'd already checked her phone once to see if he'd texted or tried to call, but had put it away again when her mother frowned in her direction. Her parents weren't fans of the current trend to have cellular phones constantly in hand. To them, parties were for socializing with the people actually at the party.

Normally, EvaMarie didn't have a problem with that. Tonight was a whole other matter, in more ways than one.

Suddenly her father announced, "I need to sit down."

Her mother assisted him with a concerned look that encouraged EvaMarie to stay close. If her father started having difficulty or limb pain while in the midst of all these watching eyes, her mother wouldn't cope well.

"I'm fine, Bev," he barked as her mother hovered over his left shoulder. "Just tired, all of a sudden. EvaMarie, get me some champagne."

Laurence half rose from his chair. "Would you like me to—"

"Nonsense," her father said in a gruff voice. "She's perfectly capable of fetching me a drink."

Concerned, EvaMarie hesitated, but her mother gave a quick nod in the direction of the bar. It wasn't until she was in line that the first inklings of unease appeared. Several feet away, Liza stood, holding the attention of a court of young ladies. EvaMarie knew them all. They'd grown up together.

What bothered her were the frequent glances in her direction, accompanied by giggles and whispering.

Despite the ache in the bottom of her stomach,

EvaMarie took a deep breath and turned slightly away to ignore them. Whatever was happening, she refused to feed the fire by granting it her attention. That was often the thing Liza was looking for—a way to be the center of attention in any given situation. She didn't need EvaMarie to accomplish that.

But the longer she stood there, the louder the giggling grew. EvaMarie didn't think the women were getting louder...they were simply getting closer. She ordered her father's drink and turned to go back to the table with relief.

But Liza had no intention of letting her escape. She'd barely taken half a dozen steps before the woman moved into her path. "EvaMarie, it's so nice to see you here," she cooed, the sugar-sweet tone grating on EvaMarie's nerves. Liza leaned forward as if to impart a secret, only she didn't really lower her voice. "Although I don't remember seeing your name on the guest list, if I recall correctly."

The women behind her giggled, reminding EvaMarie of a gaggle of geese playing follow the leader.

She wasn't going to give Liza the satisfaction of justifying her presence. It was a pointless exercise when Liza knew that EvaMarie could have arrived with any number of people here.

"I was just telling the girls about your new job," she said, her overly mascaraed eyelashes wide enough to show the whites of her eyes. Not the most flattering look, in EvaMarie's opinion.

"Yes?" she said. She was a working woman now. No point in hiding it, which she didn't want to do.

Earning her own living, learning exactly what she was capable of, left EvaMarie feeling pride—not shame. And looking at the women before her, the very epitome of unoccupied children without purpose in their lives, made her glad. This was what her parents had wanted for her when she was young. But it wasn't what she wanted. Her work at the library had given her a taste of creating meaning in her life by helping others. And as hard as the work with Mason had been, EvaMarie ended her days satisfied instead of empty.

"So you're living up there all alone?" one of the women asked over Liza's shoulder.

EvaMarie squinted. "I'm not sure what you mean."

"You know," the woman elaborated, "just the two of you in that big ol' house."

EvaMarie almost expected a *wink, wink* to be added. Was this really what they'd spent their time discussing? "There are a lot of workmen up there. I'm simply directing the renovations for the Harringtons."

"The Harringtons, huh?" Liza giggled. "But you and *Mason* are up there alone at night, right? At least, from what I saw." She glanced over her shoulder at the lemmings behind her. "Gives a whole new meaning to live-in help, if you know what I mean."

"No, I—"

Laurence appeared at her elbow. "Your father wants to know what's taking so long." He lifted the champagne flute from her hand.

"What do you think, Laurence?" Liza interjected.

"I'd bet the odds that EvaMarie is securing her job with *the Harringtons* in more ways than one."

EvaMarie felt her cheeks flush as Laurence didn't jump in to immediately defend her. Instead, he cast an inquiring look in her direction.

And even though EvaMarie knew her time with Mason wasn't like that, she couldn't stop the red hot glow from spreading down her throat and chest. "That's not what's happening at all," she choked out, even though her brain told her this wasn't junior high and she didn't need to justify herself to anyone.

"If it was me," Liza said, though her tone made it clear she'd never have to stoop that low, "well, let's just say I wouldn't blame you for milking that relationship for all it's worth. You get to hold on to your home and garner the attentions of one sexy man… although I notice he wasn't the one who brought you tonight. Now was he?"

Just like that, EvaMarie felt her innermost fears laid bare for this uncaring group to dissect and make fun of at her expense. Even Laurence, who'd always stood by her despite her decidedly outcast role in recent years, continued to eye her as if he could see all her secrets behind her fancy retro gown. Finally he asked, "Well, he certainly does have himself a sweet deal, doesn't he?"

"Laurence." Anger started to replace the nerves she felt in the pit of her stomach. "That's completely uncalled for." Regardless of whether or not it might be true. "I keep my job the same way any employee does. I work hard, and go above and beyond for the Harringtons."

"Do you now?"

Mason's voice from right behind her should have been a relief. But the hard tone didn't reassure her at all. Before she could turn, he stepped in close to her back and spoke to the others. "If you all would excuse us, please?"

Then his hand encircled her wrist, a perfect pivot for him to turn her to face him. She had a brief glimpse of Laurence's angry expression before Mason whisked her out onto the dance floor.

His sure touch guided her into a loosely modified version of a modern waltz that allowed them to slowly traverse the lightly populated space. Most people were still enjoying the hors d'oeuvres and drinks and hadn't taken advantage of the live music yet.

The glitter in Mason's blue eyes as he stared down at her didn't calm her unsettled nerves. She'd wondered how he would react to seeing her here. She was about to find out.

"So, was Laurence right? Seems to me you've gotten quite a few perks out of this deal. Though it hadn't occurred to me that you might be milking every opportunity to get exactly what you wanted... until tonight."

"I don't understand..."

"I went into your closet tonight."

Her stumble could have been disastrous, but Mason's smooth save kept them upright and floating across the floor. The whirl of the crowd on the periphery of her vision made EvaMarie a little nauseous.

As if he could read her understanding in her expression, Mason gave a nod, then went on. "So you do understand? How many other secrets have you been keeping from me?"

"What? None." This new assault from a completely unexpected direction left EvaMarie grasping for a response. "Look, I wasn't ready to talk about what I was trying to do..."

"Right." His expression turned into a glare. "It would be a shame for me to encourage you."

"Would you have?"

Mason didn't answer, just continued with his unrelenting glare. EvaMarie wasn't sure exactly what was happening here. She'd made a mistake not telling Mason about her narration job, but they really hadn't had a lot of time to build that kind of trust. Especially in a situation that had an end date in sight...

When he still didn't speak, EvaMarie gave in to her own internal pressure to explain. "I'm just trying to build some sort of career."

"A career based in my house."

His resentment was becoming clearer. "Actually, I can do it anywhere. You know as well as I do that I needed a place to stay—"

"—and work."

"And it helped to be able to continue to work, but that's not why—"

"Why you slept with me?"

The emotions that stopped EvaMarie in her tracks were too complicated to untangle. She found herself searching Mason's face, desperate for any sign of the lover and, yes, friend she'd spent the last few weeks with. The man who had let go of the need for revenge that he'd shown up with on her doorstep. "Is that really how you see me? As a woman who would sleep with you for the chance to stay in my childhood home and—" nausea tightened her throat "—get paid for it?"

In the back of her mind, she realized people were starting to watch them, listen to their conversation. And all of Liza's suspicions were being confirmed. But what mattered right now was Mason and the realization that he hadn't changed as much from that vengeful man as she'd thought.

"Well, you haven't really let me get to know you, the real you, have you? So I can't really say."

"Are you kidding me?" she asked, incredulous. "I keep one thing a secret and now I'm hiding from you? Is that how you really view me? Or is this just an excuse to push me away now that other people are starting to talk?"

"I'm not the one who's always cared what other people think. Am I?"

No, he wasn't. But that didn't really answer her question.

EvaMarie was immediately struck by the sudden awareness of how quiet the other conversations in the large room had gotten. And as much as she'd like to say she didn't care, that didn't mean she longed to air her dirty laundry in front of all of these people.

Without answering, she turned on her heel, stalking back to her parents' table. "EvaMarie," her mother said fretfully as she approached.

She ignored her, ignored her father's hard stare, ignored Laurence's arrival right after her. Instead, she reached for her clutch and shawl. She'd had enough partying for one night.

But Mason wasn't done. "So let's just get one thing straight," he said, the sound of his angry voice scraping across her nerves. "Did you or did you not work with me, sleep with me, so you could stay close to your very nice, very free studio in order to build your new career?"

"No," she snapped.

"Then why the secrecy?"

Before she could tell him to go to hell, her father bellowed, "What's he talking about?"

"Nothing."

Still he struggled to his feet, always willing to use his large stature to intimidate an answer out of her. "Why would you need a career?" he demanded. "We agreed you're taking the job with Mrs. Robinson."

"A job?" Mason's voice had gone deadly deep, shaking EvaMarie far more than her father's at his worst. Mason moved in closer, right over her shoulder. He left no space for her to turn and face him. "What? No two weeks' notice? Or do you only grant others that kind of courtesy when it suits you to do so?"

Sixteen

Mason should have been satisfied as he replayed the memory of EvaMarie running from the Young house, the fragile vintage gown pulled up away from her heels. Instead, he clenched his fists around the steering wheel and hit the gas with considerably more force.

He'd walked away from a blustering Daulton as he demanded EvaMarie tell him what was going on. Their little family drama didn't interest him. She'd run past him across the large main foyer as he'd made his apologies to Liza's parents for disrupting their party. But he had the uncomfortable feeling that the argument hadn't bothered them the way it had Mason.

After all, he'd just made them the talk of the town

without any effort. Though Lord only knew what this would do to the Harrington reputation. Probably enhance it, considering how backward things like this worked in the world.

Now he let himself into the house and paused a moment to listen to the stillness. EvaMarie's car was in the drive, not in the garage where she normally parked it.

Was she in her room? The kitchen? Was she planning to continue their discussion? Maybe offer him something special to tease him out of his bad mood?

Mason shook his head. As angry as he was, he recognized that wasn't the EvaMarie he knew. Yes, he'd lashed out and accused her of sleeping with him to get what she wanted. But deep down he didn't want to believe that could be true.

But he wasn't sure the woman he'd come to know as an adult was real. Had she been hiding behind what he wanted to see in order to hold on to the life she hadn't been ready to give up? Even worse, he wasn't sure what to do about that.

Right now, he just needed some freakin' sleep.

Only it didn't look like he was going to get it. As he approached the darkened back staircase, Mason looked up to see EvaMarie seated on one of the upper steps, a pool of frothy material puddled around her. She stared out the arched window opposite, giving him a decent view of streaked mascara and the luxurious wash of hair she'd let down to cover her bare back.

Did she have to be so lovely?

He clenched his fists, wishing he could eradicate all sympathy, all regret from his emotions right now. If only she didn't look like a Cinderella after the ball, after her world had gone to hell in a handbasket. If only she didn't make his heart ache to hold her just once more—even when he knew he shouldn't.

The silence lasted for long minutes more as he stared at her from the bottom of the stairs. Maybe he'd been wrong. Maybe she was justified in keeping her secrets. But what about the job? Or rather, the new job. That familiar anger and hurt flooded his chest once more.

Just when he'd thought she wouldn't, EvaMarie spoke. "I'll be out by Monday."

He drew in a deep breath, but she didn't give him an inch of ground.

"I'd be out sooner, but everything was going so well, I sort of forgot I was supposed to be packing."

"So did I."

And he had, because deep inside, he hadn't wanted to think about EvaMarie leaving. Because her leaving would have made him wonder why being without her left him lonely, why laughing with her made him happy and why knowing she'd kept even a small part of herself from him made him angry.

Because he'd fallen in love, all over again.

She stood, the fall of the gown reflecting the scant moonlight from the window opposite. A few steps was all she gained before she turned back. "I'm sorry, Mason. I know you probably won't believe that. Probably don't even care. But I need to say it for myself. I'm sorry that I kept things from you."

Her huff of a laugh resonated with a sort of despair that startled him. "I thought everything I'd done for you, with you, would have told you what you needed to truly know about me. But I forget that's not the way life works. It never has been. At least, not for me. I've spent a lifetime protecting myself, and old habits die hard, regardless of whether they are serving you well or not. And that's my fault."

"No, EvaMarie." Without thought he moved to the bottom of the stairs, gripping the newel post in his hand. "No, I just didn't expect—"

"That the young, innocent girl you knew would grow up into such a complicated woman. So needy. So scared." Her hand was a pale blur as she waved it to indicate the house at her feet. "After all, I had the perfect life. The least I could do was meet your expectations."

She moved down a step, then stopped to hold herself in frozen stillness as if realizing she'd made a mistake. "That's what everyone else wants. So you should too. Only I thought you wanted me to grow, wanted me to break out from my past—" her voice rose to echo around the black space "—wanted me to take what I wanted." A small sob escaped her throat. "But no one really means that. They just say it to be nice and take it back when it doesn't go the way they expected."

She turned away once more, not speaking again until she reached the top step. Mason's gaze traced the fragile line of her spine where the dress dipped to midback below the fall of her hair, remembering the feel of it against his fingertips.

Her words floated down without her turning her head toward him. "Jeremy was right. No one will ever respect me, because I don't respect myself. So from here on out, I'll accept nothing less…only I figure that means I'll spend a lifetime alone. Funny how that works, huh?"

In that moment, Mason realized he'd let EvaMarie down far worse than anything she'd ever done to him when they were kids. Then, she hadn't stood up for him because she didn't know how. Now, he'd taken advantage of the fact that she wouldn't stand up for herself to exorcise his own anger and conflicting emotions.

Guilt gripped his throat, refusing to let him call out to her as she walked away. He heard the door to her room close, then the distinct click of the lock.

She was done talking, leaving Mason to spend the night contemplating just how big of a jackass he truly was.

She's really done it.

Mason came around the corner of the house to find a long horse trailer parked before the stables. Jim came out the arched entryway leading Lucy, her foal not far behind. Somehow, seeing the horses loaded up with their new owners—without EvaMarie anywhere in sight—told Mason's brain more than anything else that she was gone.

When she'd left him a note telling him she wouldn't be back, she'd meant it.

He hadn't seen her after that night. Her room had been empty the next day, save for a stack of moving boxes in one corner and the furniture. If she had been at the house since that night, it hadn't been while Mason was present. He suspected Jeremy was helping her coordinate her movements, though the other man hadn't said a word.

All of her belongings, including her sound equipment, had been loaded into moving trucks the third day by a group of burly men in uniforms. But it still hadn't seemed real. Until the horses...

EvaMarie had loved those horses. He'd just assumed she would be here to say goodbye to them.

Kane appeared beside him. "What's going on?"

Mason bumped his chin in the direction of the stables. "New owner is here for the Hyatts' horses. Got the stables all to ourselves now."

Kane grunted. "We're gonna need to hire on some help for Jim." He was quiet again for a moment, then said the very thing Mason didn't want to hear. "You okay with this?"

"Hell, yes." But he wasn't. And that was eating away his insides.

"No," he finally conceded. "Hell, no."

Kane slapped Mason's shoulder. "About time you admitted that."

"Why? So you can gloat?"

"Would I do that?"

"Yes." And that was an understatement.

"Nah! But I might have to indulge in at least one *I told you so*."

As much as he'd like to, Mason couldn't begrudge him that. "You were right."

Kane clutched his heart in a mock death grip. "And you admitted it? Is the world ending?"

"It will for you if you don't drop the theatrics."

Kane chuckled, a sound so rare it startled Mason. "I can't resist."

"Try."

Mason frowned as Jim and the new owner checked over the inside and outside of the trailer to make sure the horses were safe and secure. "This didn't go how I thought it would."

"Life is full of surprises, Dad used to say."

"And not all of them good, if I remember correctly."

"He did mention that a time or two. And as much as you showing up here was a nasty surprise for the Hyatts, I think it was a good thing for EvaMarie."

"I doubt she'd agree with you now."

"You sure about that?"

Mason studied him.

"Do you remember the year I was in sixth grade?"

"Yeah. That was a pretty miserable year for you." It was before Kane had gotten any height on him. He'd spent the year being picked on by a particularly burly boy at school. "Why?"

"I learned something that year. Oh, I didn't learn it right then. But many years later, looking back, I was taught a massive life lesson."

"That bullies need their asses kicked?"

Kane smirked. "Besides that. I learned that the job of a bully is to make you cower. Not just outside, but inside. To make everything you are shrink until it disappears, including the very essence of who you are."

Mason could see where this was going, and it wasn't helping him feel any better.

"EvaMarie lived with a bully her entire life," Kane went on. "The thing that amazes me to this day is the amount of strength it took for her not to give up, not to lose who she really was. She buried it, and protected it, until the time when it was safe for her to bring it back out."

"So I could stomp all over it." Mason watched the truck and trailer disappear down the drive. Jim raised a hand in acknowledgment before heading back into the stables. They really had to get that man some help. "I completely screwed up. How do I change that?"

"It's easy…"

"For you to say."

Kane squinted as he gazed across the rolling hills behind the stable yard. "Nope. You've just got to help her be who she should have been all along."

Seventeen

"Jeremy, come on," EvaMarie hollered. She couldn't help it. Wondering if Mason was gonna walk in at any minute had her stomach cramping.

Jeremy finally came around the corner from the basement with a grin that made her want to smack him. "Seriously, you could at least be curious as to how the game room turned out."

Oh, she was. More than anything she wanted to take a leisurely stroll downstairs to see all the cool goodness Jeremy had been able to put in place. She wanted to see how the plans they had all discussed and dreamed about had come to life... She wanted to see how the furniture she and Mason had picked out looked in the game room. She wanted to talk party plans and food and music…but that wasn't her place anymore.

"I just want to get my stuff from the safe and go," she insisted, ignoring what she wanted but could no longer have.

"Well, why didn't you go on up and get it?"

Because it was weird.

She knew Mason had now moved the focus of the renovations to the second floor. Honestly, she'd be surprised if he hadn't gutted her room. He probably wanted absolutely nothing to remind him of her. Probably the entire floor was unrecognizable now. What had they done with Chris's bedroom? The thought left her cold. She wasn't sure she wanted to see.

Jeremy watched her closely, seeming almost amused. "I told you Mason left the safe on purpose once I explained you'd forgotten some things in it."

"I'm amazed he didn't blow it out of the wall," she mumbled.

"Oh, stop fussing and get a move on."

She totally wasn't in the mood for his attitude. "Now who's in a hurry?" she challenged.

But she did want to get done before Mason arrived. In the three weeks since she'd left her childhood home, she hadn't seen Mason once. Not driving around town, not out shopping and certainly not here at the estate.

The few times she'd returned for her things, Jeremy had arranged for her to show up when Mason wasn't home. Whether her former lover approved of this strategy or not, she wasn't sure. When she realized that she'd forgotten to get the few real pieces of jewelry she still owned from the wall safe in her closet, it had taken a whole week for Jeremy to find a window for her to come by.

But standing around here in the hall that had seen all the ups and downs in her life made her sink even further into the morass of sadness that darkened her life at the moment. She needed out. As a matter of fact, she almost gave Jeremy the code and asked him to get her stuff from the safe, but she'd done enough wimping out for the day. This she needed to do for herself.

Hard as it might be.

So she forced herself to climb each step, focusing on Jeremy's leather shoes at her eye level in front of her. They shouldn't be so fancy for all the work he did in construction zones, but somehow he managed to pull it off without a single scuff. Amazing.

With a grimace, she acknowledged that she was in deep avoidance mode, but she still refused to look right or left as she crossed the landing to her old room. Her brother's room pulled at her senses, but what good would looking do? He was gone. So was her childhood. Wandering these halls to reminisce about either would probably throw her into a depression she could never crawl out of.

"How are the parents?" Jeremy asked, as he paused outside the door to her old bedroom.

"Currently refusing to speak to me," she confirmed. "Once I told them they could agree to my terms or not see me, they immediately set about breaking every rule I put in place. We're in what I call the tantrum stage."

"Ah, the terrible twos."

"And threes and fours and fives... I feel like it's never going to end."

"It will."

"I hate to say it, but I agree. The minute my dad has his first big health scare and they need me, they'll come calling. I'll just have to remind them that I mean business on a regular basis." Just the thought exhausted her sometimes, but this was life with her parents, since she wasn't willing to cut them out altogether.

Jeremy echoed her thoughts. "I know it's hard, but stick to your guns."

She hated to admit it, but being away from her parents right now was easier than going along with all their demands had ever been. But remembering that would help her keep her backbone strong. It would have been nice to have someone by her side, giving her encouragement and support while she dealt with all of this, but she'd lost that chance the night of the ball.

Without voicing her complicated thoughts, she nodded. "All right. Let's see it."

Jeremy opened the door and stood aside, telling her something had definitely changed beyond the threshold. As much as she dreaded it, this was another good thing. A hard thing, but she needed to remember that this was no longer her home. The past was gone. She couldn't go back.

Especially now that her room had been turned into an office. Her first thought was that it had been turned into Mason's office, but the pale purple of the walls didn't really scream "masculine." With a quick glance, she scanned what appeared to be an antique rolltop desk, a modern ergonomic desk chair covered in a leather that matched the desk's finish and some bookshelves. She didn't look closer. She didn't want to.

Definitely not.

The pale purple had been carried over into the dressing room, but unlike the other space, this one remained unfurnished. Then she opened the door to the walk-in closet and gasped.

Instead of the stripped walls she'd expected, all the surfaces had been reinforced with cushioning covered in some kind of leather. Decorative tufting had been created with upholstery buttons. At the far end, a custom-built shelving unit and desk took up the entire wall. An L-shaped addition on one side was filled with equipment that made the woman who had poured over sound equipment sites to find the best of the cheapest drool.

"Oh my God, Jeremy," she breathed.

"Do you like it?"

That deep voice wasn't Jeremy's. Barely able to breathe, EvaMarie turned in a slow circle until she faced Mason in the doorway. A remote part of her brain recognized that she'd started to shake, but the rest of her was simply working to keep herself upright.

"Um…" *Oh, real intelligent, EvaMarie.* "It's wonderful."

He stepped farther inside, sending a jolt through EvaMarie's core that she struggled to hide. When his gaze narrowed, she wasn't sure she'd succeeded.

"I'm glad you like it," he said, that deep, soothing tone gliding over her like a calming wave. "I did it with you in mind."

Um, thanks? She could have happily gone years without knowing that she'd inspired a room in his house. Was he crazy? "I don't know what to say," she murmured.

"Say you'll use it to record that sexy voice for me and the world to listen to."

She must not have heard him right. "What?" she gasped.

"I built it for you, EvaMarie."

She could swear she'd heard him wrong, but the acoustics in here were excellent. Perfect for her business. "I lined up two new authors this week," she said, the inane trivia the only thing her brain could cough up. Then she winced. Her "career" was probably the last thing he wanted to hear about.

"That's because you're excellent at everything you put your mind to," Mason said, surprising her.

A deep breath helped her gather the unraveling threads of her cognitive abilities. "That's what you said the last time I saw you. That I'm as good at secrets and lies as I am at cleaning up after the construction crew."

"And this is my way of saying I'm sorry."

She glanced around the impressive space, awed for a moment. "Pretty expensive apology."

"It's worth every penny if it means you'll at least talk to me again."

"Again…it seems like a lot for talking." She just couldn't let it go.

"You're gonna have to grovel, my man!"

"Go away, Jeremy!" Mason yelled back toward the bedroom. "I don't need an audience."

EvaMarie struggled not to smile. What had happened between them wasn't funny, but her emotions were never straightforward with this man. But confusion quickly overtook all her other thoughts.

She shook her head. "I don't understand."

"Understand what?" Mason took a step closer, which didn't clear her thoughts at all.

"I mean, I really don't understand. You hate my family. You hate what I let them do to me. You think I was using you for a place to live and work." She stepped back, struggling to breathe. "After all that, why would you do this?"

Tears threatened to surface. What she'd wanted all along seemed right within her reach, but she couldn't take it, because she couldn't live with him thinking of her that way.

"Remember, we said no other rules. Right?"

Not trusting herself to speak, she nodded.

"Well, I was wrong. There is a third rule."

"What's that?"

"We have to respect each other."

And just like that, her heart shattered. Mason would never respect the woman he thought she was.

"Do you respect me, EvaMarie?"

That was easy. She'd seen the man he'd become— a fierce opponent when fighting what he believed was wrong, utterly loyal and still as hardworking as he had been when he was young. "Of course."

"Even with my faults?"

She'd had enough time to get some perspective on that. "We all make mistakes." Hadn't she?

"And I more than most." This time he moved in close, not giving her a chance to back down. "I built this room to show you that I respect and support the woman you are now." His hands gripped her upper arms, anchoring her to the reality of what he was saying. "The woman who takes the time to read to children, who isn't afraid of hard work or to challenge me when I'm being a total ass."

She tried to smother her grin, but he caught it anyway, shared it with her despite the seriousness of what he said.

"The woman who pays attention to details, and sings to calm the horses. The woman who, even now, is struggling to teach her parents better manners while refusing to abandon them in their time of need."

"Jeremy told you?"

Mason nodded. "He told me. And I'm proud of you."

With that, she could no longer hold back the tears.

Ever so gently, Mason tilted her chin up so her watery gaze could meet his. "Let me be the first to say, EvaMarie, that I'm very proud of you. I know it's not easy. You could have continued to keep the status quo, but you saw that it wasn't the best thing for any of you, and you did something about it."

EvaMarie couldn't explain how his words made her feel. It wasn't just love. It wasn't just about soaking in the rare bit of praise. It was her heart blossoming as she realized someone could get her for the first time—warts and all.

"So you want to, what? Go back to how we were before?" She wasn't sure that's what she wanted anymore.

He buried his hand in her hair, bringing that sculpted mouth so close to hers. "Oh, I want what we had before…but I want much, much more."

His kiss left her reeling, so it was hard to coordinate her feet when he pulled her back toward the door. When they reached the office, she saw a dress hanging from one of the bookshelves. "That wasn't there before."

"Nope."

It was a vintage style with a close-fitting bodice and a full, frilly skirt. The crisp teal cotton was complemented by the lace-edged crinoline beneath the skirt. On the shelf above was a stylish hat with a matching teal ribbon woven through the brim.

EvaMarie pressed her palm hard against her stomach to quiet the butterflies that had taken up residence there. "What's that for?"

"Well, I was hoping you'd still help us with our open house when we put it on."

Her heart sank, and it was a literal, physical feeling. She eyed the dress with longing, wishing it represented so much more than it appeared to.

"As my fiancée."

Turning to look at Mason, EvaMarie found him on one knee right there in her old bedroom. His hand was lifted up to reveal a gorgeous white gold and amethyst ring with a circlet of tiny diamonds supporting it. "Mason?"

"I don't want there to be any more misunderstanding between us, EvaMarie. We're both products of our upbringing, but we're our own people too. And personally, I think you've turned into something incredible. Can you forgive me for letting the past get in the way of the present?"

Heart aching, she stepped in close, pulling his head to her chest. "Only if you can help me be the person I should be."

Mason looked up to meet her gaze. "No, but I can help you be the person *you want* to be."

Standing, he kissed her again with a soft reverence that made her heart ache. Then he pulled her close against his body. As she looked over his shoulder, the pictures on the bookshelves became clear for the first time. Framed pictures of her and her brother. "Mason, how?"

"Jeremy got them out of storage for me. I never

want you to feel like you can't talk about your life. All the parts of it."

"I promise this time I will."

Mason scanned the busy rooms on each side of the hall, looking for his fiancée in the midst of the open house chaos. People stopped him frequently. He had to consciously tamp down his impatience with the interruptions. They'd staged this party to make themselves known and extend memorable hospitality.

Mason would just enjoy it more with EvaMarie by his side.

His hunting skills proved apt when he tracked her to the kitchen. There she was in her gorgeous dress, busily helping the caterer fill trays. He watched her for several long moments.

She wasn't anything like he'd expected when he'd shown up at the estate that first day. Instead, she was more.

"Woman, what are you doing?" he finally asked.

She glanced up, giving him a glimpse of her round blue eyes beneath the rim of her hat before dusting off her fingers. "I'm sorry, Mason. I just worry about everything getting done."

Secretly he was amused, but he couldn't resist the blush staining her cheeks. He stepped closer, running his knuckles lightly down the flushed skin. "I understand. But you're the lady of the house. And this dress is not meant for the kitchen."

They left the room to the chorus of giggles from the catering crew. "When you said you weren't big on parties, I thought you were just saying that because of the last time you went to one," Mason said as he led her through the people meandering between the front rooms and the hopping activities in the basement.

"Honestly, I've never been big on them. Not nearly as much as my parents," she murmured, sticking close to his side. Mason was amazed at how good that felt. "I'd much rather be upstairs with a book."

The turret library had been bumped to the front of the restoration checklist. They'd returned a large number of EvaMarie's books there, along with Mason's own smaller collection. They spent a lot of quiet evenings in that room, before Mason coaxed her down to the master suite.

He snuggled her closer to his side, bending to her ear to say, "As much as I was looking forward to this event, I'd rather be upstairs too...for a completely different reason."

She gasped as he whisked her partway up the stairs. "Mason, we can't."

A quick maneuver and she was in his arms as they looked out across their guests. Sunlight from the arched window opposite highlighted her cheekbones, reminding Mason of the angel he'd allowed into his life. "I'm teasing you, Evie," he said, grinning at her knowing look.

She knew him all too well.

A particularly loud guffaw had Mason glancing toward the ballroom, which they could see a sliver of from their elevated position. EvaMarie's parents held court in one corner of the room. "Your father is in his element."

"Amazingly." EvaMarie shook her head. "I can't believe they're actually here."

Mason had done his best to support her as she struggled to establish her relationship with her parents on a new footing. There'd been many a time he'd wanted to step in, but he rarely had to do that. EvaMarie, perfectionist that she was, knew exactly what she wanted and stuck to her guns in order to get it.

"You did it, love," he said, kissing her temple. "The house is gorgeous, the party is a hit and your career is gaining momentum. I'm damn proud."

"Thank you."

The tight squeeze of her arms conveyed her heightened emotions. Mason continued to be amazed when she admitted she needed help from him. The admissions were few and far between, but each one made him feel like a superhero as he attempted to give back even a fraction of the support she granted him every day.

"Where's your brother?" she asked.

Mason swept his gaze over the floor once more. "He must still be at the stables. There was a problem getting the stud settled in."

She nodded. "Soon the stables will be set—"

"And we will be the newest stables to win a Kentucky Derby. Just you see."

Her smile gave him the biggest boost. "I'm sure I will."

"It's gonna be beautiful. Just like you."

"No," she said, leaning her head against his chest. "Like us together."

* * * * *

*If you loved this book, pick up
the* MILL TOWN MILLIONAIRES *novels
from Dani Wade*

*A BRIDE'S TANGLED VOWS
THE BLACKSTONE HEIR
THE RENEGADE RETURNS
EXPECTING HIS SECRET HEIR*

*And don't miss Dani's first Harlequin Desire
HIS BY DESIGN*

***

*If you're on Twitter, tell us what you think
of Harlequin Desire! #harlequindesire*

If you like sexy and steamy stories with strong heroines and irresistible heroes, you'll love FORGED IN DESIRE by New York Times *bestselling author Brenda Jackson—featuring Margo Connelly and Lamar "Striker" Jennings, the reformed bad boy who'll do anything to protect her, even if it means lowering the defenses around his own heart...*

Turn the page for a sneak peek at FORGED IN DESIRE!

PROLOGUE

"FINALLY, WE GET to go home."

Margo Connelly was certain the man's words echoed the sentiment they all felt. The last thing she'd expected when reporting for jury duty was to be sequestered during the entire trial...especially with twelve strangers, more than a few of whom had taken the art of bitching to a whole new level.

She was convinced this had been the longest, if not the most miserable, six weeks of her life, as well as a lousy way to start off the new year. They hadn't been allowed to have any inbound or outbound calls, read the newspapers, check any emails, watch television or listen to the radio. The only good thing was, with the vote just taken, a unanimous decision had been reached and justice would be served. The federal case against Murphy Erickson would finally be over and they would be allowed to go home.

"It's time to let the bailiff know we've reached a decision," Nancy Snyder spoke up, interrupting Margo's thoughts. "I have a man waiting at home, who I haven't seen in six weeks, and I can't wait to get to him."

Lucky you, Margo thought, leaning back in her

chair. She and Scott Dylan had split over a year ago, and the parting hadn't been pretty.

Fortunately, as a wedding-dress designer, she could work from anywhere and had decided to move back home to Charlottesville. She could be near her uncle Frazier, her father's brother and the man who'd become her guardian when her parents had died in a house fire when she was ten. He was her only living relative and, although they often butted heads, she had missed him while living in New York.

A knock on the door got everyone's attention. The bailiff had arrived. Hopefully, in a few hours it would all be over and the judge would release them. She couldn't wait to get back to running her business. Six weeks had been a long time away. Lucky for her she had finished her last order in time for the bride's Christmas wedding. But she couldn't help wondering how many new orders she might have missed while on jury duty.

The bailiff entered and said, "The judge has called the court back in session for the reading of the verdict. We're ready to escort you there."

Like everyone else in the room, Margo stood. She was ready for the verdict to be read. It was only after this that she could get her life back.

"FOREMAN, HAS THE jury reached a verdict?" the judge asked.

"Yes, we have, Your Honor."

The courtroom was quiet as the verdict was read.

"We, the jury, find Murphy Erickson guilty of murder."

Suddenly Erickson bowled over and laughed. It made the hairs on the necks of everyone in attendance stand up. The outburst prompted the judge to hit his gavel several times. "Order in the courtroom. Counselor, quiet the defendant or he will be found in contempt of court."

"I don't give a damn about any contempt," Erickson snarled loudly. "You!" he said, pointing a finger at the judge. "Along with everyone else in this courtroom, you have just signed your own death warrant. As long as I remain locked up, someone in here will die every seventy-two hours." His gaze didn't miss a single individual.

Pandemonium broke out. The judge pounded his gavel, trying to restore order. Police officers rushed forward to subdue Erickson and haul him away. But the sound of his threats echoed loudly in Margo's ears.

CHAPTER ONE

LAMAR "STRIKER" JENNINGS walked into the hospital room, stopped and then frowned. "What the hell is he doing working from bed?"

"I asked myself the same thing when I got his call for us to come here," Striker's friend Quasar Patterson said, sitting lazily in a chair with his long legs stretched out in front of him.

"And you might as well take a seat like he told us to do," another friend, Stonewall Courson, suggested, while pointing to an empty chair. "Evidently it will take more than a bullet to slow down Roland."

Roland Summers, CEO of Summers Security Firm, lay in the hospital bed, staring at them. Had it been just last week that the man had been fighting for his life after foiling an attempted carjacking?

"You still look like shit, Roland. Shouldn't you be trying to get some rest instead of calling a meeting?" Striker asked, sliding his tall frame into the chair. He didn't like seeing Roland this way. They'd been friends a long time, and he couldn't ever recall the man being sick. Not even with a cold. Well, at least he was alive. That damn bullet could have taken him out and Striker didn't want to think about that.

"You guys have been keeping up with the news?" Roland asked in a strained voice, interrupting Striker's thoughts.

"We're aware of what's going on, if that's what you want to know," Stonewall answered. "Nobody took Murphy Erickson's threat seriously."

Roland made an attempt to nod his head. "And now?"

"And now people are panicking. Phones at the office have been ringing off the hook. I'm sure every protective security service in town is booked solid. Everyone in the courtroom that day is either in hiding or seeking protection, and with good reason," Quasar piped in to say. "The judge, clerk reporter and bailiff are all dead. All three were gunned down within seventy-two hours of each other."

"The FBI is working closely with local law enforcement, and they figure it's the work of the same assassin," Striker added. "I heard they anticipate he'll go after someone on the jury next."

"Which is why I called the three of you here. There was a woman on the jury who I want protected. It's personal."

"Personal?" Striker asked, lifting a brow. He knew Roland dated off and on, but he'd never been serious with anyone. He was always quick to say that his wife, Becca, had been his one and only love.

"Yes, personal. She's a family member."

The room got quiet. That statement was even more baffling since, as far as the three of them knew, Roland didn't have any family...at least not anymore.

They were all aware of his history. He'd been a cop, who'd discovered some of his fellow officers on the take. Before he could blow the whistle he'd been framed and sent to prison for fifteen years. Becca had refused to accept his fate and worked hard to get him a new trial. He served three years before finally leaving prison but not before the dirty cops murdered Roland's wife. All the cops involved had eventually been brought to justice and charged with the death of Becca Summers, in addition to other crimes.

"You said she's family?" Striker asked, looking confused.

"Yes, although I say that loosely since we've never officially met. I know who she is, but she doesn't know I even exist." Roland then closed his eyes, and Striker knew he had to be in pain.

"Man, you need to rest," Quasar spoke up. "You can cover this with us another time."

Roland's eyes flashed back open. "No, we need to talk now. I need one of you protecting her right away."

Nobody said anything for a minute and then Striker asked, "What relation is she to you, man?"

"My niece. To make a long story short, years ago my mom got involved with a married man. He broke things off when his wife found out about the affair but not before I was conceived. I always knew the identity of my father. I also knew about his other two, older sons, although they didn't know about me. I guess you can say I was the old man's secret.

"One day after I'd left for college, I got a call from

my mother letting me know the old man was dead but he'd left me something in his will."

Striker didn't say anything, thinking that at least Roland's old man had done right by him in the end. To this day, his own poor excuse of a father hadn't even acknowledged his existence. "That's when your two brothers found out about you?" he asked.

"Yes. Their mother found out about me, as well. She turned out to be a real bitch. Even tried blocking what Connelly had left for me in the will. But she couldn't. The old man evidently had anticipated her making such a move and made sure the will was ironclad. He gave me enough to finish college without taking out student loans with a little left over."

"Good for him," Quasar said. "What about your brothers? How did they react to finding out about you?"

"The eldest acted like a dickhead," Roland said without pause. "The other one's reaction was just the opposite. His name was Murdock and he reached out to me afterward. I would hear from him from time to time. He would call to see how I was doing."

Roland didn't say anything for a minute, his face showing he was struggling with strong emotions. "Murdock is the one who gave Becca the money to hire a private investigator to reopen my case. I never got the chance to thank him."

"Why?" Quasar asked.

Roland drew in a deep breath and then said, "Murdock and his wife were killed weeks before my new trial began."

"How did they die?"

"House fire. Fire department claimed faulty wiring. I never believed it but couldn't prove otherwise. Luckily their ten-year-old daughter wasn't home at the time. She'd been attending a sleepover at one of her friends' houses."

"You think those dirty cops took them out, too?" Stonewall asked.

"Yes. While I could link Becca's death to those corrupt cops, there wasn't enough evidence to connect Murdock's and his wife's deaths."

Stonewall nodded. "What happened to the little girl after that?"

"She was raised by the other brother. Since the old lady had died by then, he became her guardian." Roland paused a minute and then added, "He came to see me this morning."

"Who? Your brother? The dickhead?" Quasar asked with a snort.

"Yes," Roland said, and it was obvious he was trying not to grin. "When he walked in here it shocked the hell out of me. Unlike Murdock, he never reached out to me, and I think he even resented Murdock for doing so."

"So what the fuck was his reason for showing up here today?" Stonewall asked. "He'd heard you'd gotten shot and wanted to show some brotherly concern?" It was apparent by Stonewall's tone he didn't believe that was the case.

"Umm, let me guess," Quasar then said languidly. "He had a change of heart, especially now that his niece's life is in danger. Now he wants your help. I assume this is the same niece you want protected."

"Yes, to both. He'd heard I'd gotten shot and claimed he was concerned. Although he's not as much of a dickhead as before, I sensed a little resentment is still there. But not because I'm his father's bastard—a part of me believes he's gotten over that."

"What, then?" Striker asked.

"I think he blames me for Murdock's death. He didn't come out and say that, but he did let me know he was aware of the money Murdock gave Becca to get me a new trial and that he has similar suspicions regarding the cause of their deaths. That's why, when he became his niece's guardian, he sent her out of the country to attend an all-girls school with tight security in London for a few years. He didn't bring her back to the States until after those bad cops were sent to jail."

"So the reason he showed up today was because he thought sending you on a guilt trip would be the only way to get you to protect your niece?" Striker asked angrily. Although Roland had tried hiding it, Striker could clearly see the pain etched in his face whenever he spoke.

"Evidently. I guess it didn't occur to him that making sure she is protected is something I'd want to do. I owe Murdock, although I don't owe Frazier Connelly a damn thing."

"Frazier Connelly?" Quasar said, sitting up straight in his chair. "*The* Frazier Connelly of Connelly Enterprises?"

"One and the same."

Nobody said anything for a while. Then Striker asked, "Your niece—what's her name?"

"Margo. Margo Connelly."

"And she doesn't know anything about you?" Stonewall asked. "Are you still the family's well-kept secret?"

Roland nodded. "Frazier confirmed that today, and I prefer things to stay that way. If I could, I would protect her. I can't, so I need one of you to do it for me. Hopefully, it won't be long before the assassin that Erickson hired is apprehended."

Striker eased out of his chair. Roland, of all people, knew that, in addition to working together, he, Quasar and Stonewall were the best of friends. They looked out for each other and watched each other's back. And if needed they would cover Roland's back, as well. Roland was more than just their employer—he was their close friend, mentor and the voice of reason, even when they really didn't want one. "Stonewall is handling things at the office in your absence, and Quasar is already working a case. That leaves me. Don't worry about a thing, Roland. I've got it covered. Consider it done."

MARGO CONNELLY STARED up at her uncle. "A bodyguard? Do you really think that's necessary, Uncle Frazier? I understand extra policemen are patrolling the streets."

"That's not good enough. Why should I trust a bunch of police officers?"

"Why shouldn't you?" she countered, not for the first time wondering what her uncle had against cops.

"I have my reasons, but this isn't about me—this is about you and your safety. I refuse to have you placed in any danger. What's the big deal? You've had a bodyguard before."

Yes, she'd had one before. Right after her parents' deaths, when her uncle had become her guardian. He had shipped her off to London for three years. She'd reckoned he'd been trying to figure out what he, a devout bachelor, was to do with a ten-year-old. When she returned to the United States, Apollo remained her bodyguard. When she turned fourteen, she fought hard for a little personal freedom. But she'd always known the chauffeurs Uncle Frazier hired could do more than drive her to and from school. More than once she'd seen the guns they carried.

"Yes, but that was then and this is now, Uncle Frazier. I can look after myself."

"Haven't you been keeping up with the news?" he snapped. "Three people are dead. All three were in that courtroom with you. Erickson is making sure his threat is carried out."

"And more than likely whoever is committing these murders will be caught before there can be another shooting. I understand the three were killed while they were away from home. I have enough paperwork to catch up on here for a while. I didn't even leave my house today."

"You don't think a paid assassin will find you here? Alone? You either get on board with having a bodyguard or you move back home. It's well secured there."

Margo drew in a deep breath. Back home was the Connelly estate. Yes, it was secure, with its state-of-the-art surveillance system. While growing up, she'd thought of the ten-acre property, surrounded by a tall wrought iron fence and cameras watching her every move, as a prison. Now she couldn't stand the thought of staying there for any long period of time…especially if Liz was still in residence.

Margo's forty-five-year-old uncle had never married and claimed he had his reasons for never wanting to. But that didn't keep him from occasionally having a live-in mistress under his roof. His most recent was Liz Tillman and, as far as Margo was concerned, the woman was a *gold digger*.

"It's final. A bodyguard will be here around the clock to protect you until this madness is over."

Margo didn't say anything. She wondered if at any time it had crossed her uncle's mind that they were at her house, not his, and she was no longer a child but a twenty-six-year-old woman. In a way she knew she should appreciate his concern, but she refused to let anyone order her around.

He was wrong in assuming she hadn't been keeping up with the news. Just because she was trying to maintain a level head didn't mean a part of her wasn't a little worried.

She frowned as she glanced up at him. The last thing she wanted was for him to worry needlessly about her. "I'll give this bodyguard a try…but he better be forewarned not to get underfoot. I have a lot of work to do." She wasn't finished yet. "And another thing, Uncle Frazier," she said, crossing her arms over her chest. "I think you forget sometimes that I'm twenty-six and live on my own. Just because I'm going along with you on this, I hope you don't think you can start bulldozing your way with me."

He glowered at her. "You're stubborn like your father."

She smiled. "I'll take that as a compliment." Dropping her hands, she moved back toward the sofa and sat down, grabbing a magazine off the coffee table to flip through. "So, when do we hire this bodyguard?"

"He's been hired. In fact, I expect him to arrive in a few minutes."

Margo's head jerked up. "What?"

Find out what happens when Margo and Striker come face-to-face in FORGED IN DESIRE by New York Times bestselling author Brenda Jackson.

Available February 2017 from Brenda Jackson and HQN Books.

*Desperate to escape her sheltered life, Hayley Thompson
quits her job as church secretary to become personal
assistant to bad-tempered, reclusive, way-too-sexy
Jonathan Bear. But his kiss is more temptation than
she bargained for!*

Read on for a sneak peek at
SEDUCE ME, COWBOY
the latest in Maisey Yates's New York Times *bestselling*
COPPER RIDGE *series!*

This was a mistake. Jonathan Bear was absolutely certain
of it. But he had earned millions making mistakes, so
what was one more? Nobody else had responded to his
ad.

Except for this pale, strange little creature who looked
barely twenty and wore the outfit of an eighty-year-old
woman.

She was… Well, she wasn't the kind of formidable
woman who could stand up to the rigors of working with
him.

His sister, Rebecca, would say—with absolutely no
tact at all—that he sucked as a boss. And maybe she was
right, but he didn't really care. He was busy, and right
now he hated most of what he was busy with.

There was irony in that, he knew. He had worked
hard all his life. He had built everything he had, brick by

brick. And every brick built a stronger wall against all the things he had left behind. Poverty, uncertainty, the lack of respect.

Finally, Jonathan Bear, that poor Indian kid who wasn't worth anything to anyone, bastard son of the biggest bastard in town, had his house on the side of the mountain and more money than he would ever be able to spend.

And he was bored out of his mind.

Boredom, it turned out, worked him into a hell of a temper. He had a feeling Hayley Thompson wasn't strong enough to stand up to that. But he expected to go through a few assistants before he found one who could handle it. She might as well be number one.

"You've got the job," he said. "You can start tomorrow."

Her eyes widened, and he noticed they were a strange shade of blue. Gray in some lights, shot through with a dark, velvet navy that reminded him of the ocean before a storm. It made him wonder if there was some hidden strength there.

They would both find out.

Don't miss
SEDUCE ME, COWBOY
by New York Times *bestselling author Maisey Yates,
available November 2016 wherever
Harlequin® Desire books and ebooks are sold.*

www.Harlequin.com

EXCLUSIVE LIMITED TIME OFFER AT
www.HARLEQUIN.com

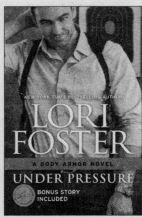

$7.99 U.S./$9.99 CAN.

$1.⁰⁰ OFF

New York Times Bestselling Author
LORI FOSTER

introduces an explosive new series
featuring sexy bodyguards who'll do
anything to protect the ones they love.

UNDER PRESSURE

He can protect anything
except his heart.

Available January 24, 2017!
Get your copy today!

Receive $1.00 OFF the purchase price of
UNDER PRESSURE by Lori Foster
when you use the coupon code below on Harlequin.com.

UPFOSTER1

Offer valid from January 24, 2017, until February 28, 2017, on www.Harlequin.com.

Valid in the U.S.A. and Canada only. To redeem this offer, please add the print or ebook version of UNDER PRESSURE by Lori Foster to your shopping cart and then enter the coupon code at checkout.

HQN™
www.HQNBooks.com

PHCOUPLFD0217

New York Times bestselling author

TAWNY WEBER

introduces the **SEAL Brotherhood**, a sizzling new series
featuring the Poseidon team—a group of hard-bodied,
fiercely competitive navy SEALs.

*When a sensitive mission goes disastrously
wrong, three of the team's finest will
have to trust their hearts and instincts to
uncover the truth…*

"No man left behind" is inscribed in the
DNA of every SEAL, and Lieutenant
Diego Torres is no exception. But with
a team member killed—and the body
missing—Diego's honor is sorely tested.
Now his career and reputation are on
the line, and a traitor is hiding among
them. Diego wants answers…and only
one woman has them.

Single mom Harper Maclean has two
priorities: raising her son, Nathan, and
starting a new life. Her mysterious new neighbor may be impossibly
charming, but Diego asks too many questions about her past—and
about the father of her child. Questions she fears will reveal her
burning attraction for Diego, and ultimately put them all in danger's path.

Includes bonus story
NIGHT MANEUVERS

Available January 31!

Order your copy today.